THE
THIRTEENTH
WARRIOR

Also by Michael Crichton

Fiction

THE ANDROMEDA STRAIN
THE TERMINAL MAN
THE GREAT TRAIN ROBBERY
CONGO
SPHERE
JURASSIC PARK
RISING SUN
DISCLOSURE
A CASE OF NEED
THE LOST WORLD
AIRFRAME

Non-fiction

FIVE PATIENTS
JASPER JOHN
ELECTRONIC LIFE
TRAVELS

THE THIRTEENTH WARRIOR

(formerly titled EATERS OF THE DEAD)

The Manuscript of Ibn Fadlan,
Relating His Experiences with
the Northmen in A.D. 922

Michael Crichton

Published by Century in 1999

1 3 5 7 9 10 8 6 4 2

The material contained in the first three chapters is substantially derived from the
manuscript of Ibn Fadlan as translated by Robert P. Blake and Richard N. Frye, and by
Albert Stanburrough Cook. Their scholarly work is gratefully acknowledged

First published in the United Kingdom in 1976 by Jonathan Cape Ltd
This edition published by Century
The Random House Group Limited
20 Vauxhall Bridge Road, London, SW1V 2SA

Random House Australia (Pty) Limited
20 Alfred Street, Milsons Point, Sydney,
New South Wales 2061, Australia

Random House New Zealand Limited
18 Poland Road, Glenfield
Auckland 10, New Zealand

Random House South Africa (Pty) Limited
Endulini, 5A Jubilee Road, Parktown 2193, South Africa

The Random House Group Limited Reg. No. 954009

www.randomhouse.co.uk

A CIP catalogue record for this book is available
from the British Library

Papers used by Random House are natural, recyclable products made from
wood grown in sustainable forests. The manufacturing processes conform
to the environmental regulations of the country of origin

ISBN 0 7126 8438 7

Typeset by SX Composing DTP, Rayleigh, Essex
Printed and bound in Great Britain by
Redwood Books, Trowbridge, Wilts.

To William Howells

"*Praise not the day until evening
has come; a woman until she is
burnt; a sword until it is tried;
a maiden until she is married;
ice until it has been crossed;
beer until it has been drunk.*"

——VIKING PROVERB

"*Evil is of old date.*"

——ARAB PROVERB

INTRODUCTION

The Ibn Fadlan manuscript represents the earliest known eyewitness account of Viking life and society. It is an extraordinary document, describing in vivid detail events which occurred more than a thousand years ago. The manuscript has not, of course, survived intact over that enormous span of time. It has a peculiar history of its own, and one no less remarkable than the text itself.

PROVENANCE OF THE MANUSCRIPT

In June, A.D. 921, the Caliph of Bagdad sent a member of his court, Ahmad Ibn Fadlan, as ambassador to the King of the Bulgars. Ibn Fadlan was gone three years on his journey and never actually accomplished his mission, for along the way he encountered a company of Norsemen and had many adventures among them.

When he finally returned to Bagdad, Ibn Fadlan re-

Introduction

corded his experiences in the form of an official report to the court. That original manuscript has long since disappeared, and to reconstruct it we must rely on partial fragments preserved in later sources.

The best-known of these is an Arabic geographical lexicon written by Yakut ibn-Abdallah sometime in the thirteenth century. Yakut includes a dozen verbatim passages from Ibn Fadlan's account, which was then three hundred years old. One must presume Yakut worked from a copy of the original. Nevertheless these few paragraphs have been endlessly translated and retranslated by later scholars.

Another fragment was discovered in Russia in 1817 and was published in German by the St. Petersburg Academy in 1823. This material includes certain passages previously published by J. L. Rasmussen in 1814. Rasmussen worked from a manuscript he found in Copenhagen, since lost, and of dubious origins. There were also Swedish, French, and English translations at this time, but they are all notoriously inaccurate and apparently do not include any new material.

In 1878, two new manuscripts were discovered in the private antiquities collection of Sir John Emerson, the British ambassador in Constantinople. Sir John was apparently one of those avid collectors whose zeal for acquisition exceeded his interest in the particular item acquired. The manuscripts were found after his death; no one knows where he obtained them, or when.

One is a geography in Arabic by Ahmad Tusi, reliably dated at A.D. 1047. This makes the Tusi manuscript chronologically closer than any other to the original of Ibn Fadlan,

2

which was presumably written around A.D. 924–926. Yet scholars regard the Tusi manuscript as the least trustworthy of all the sources; the text is full of obvious errors and internal inconsistencies, and although it quotes at length from one "Ibn Faqih" who visited the North country, many authorities hesitate to accept this material.

The second manuscript is that of Amin Razi, dating roughly from A.D. 1585–1595. It is written in Latin and according to its author is translated directly from the Arabic text of Ibn Fadlan. The Razi manuscript contains some material about the Oguz Turks, and several passages concerning battles with the mist monsters, not found in other sources.

In 1934, a final text in Medieval Latin was found in the monastery of Xymos, near Thessalonika in northeastern Greece. The Xymos manuscript contains further commentary on Ibn Fadlan's relations with the Caliph, and his experiences with the creatures of the North country. The author and date of the Xymos manuscript are both uncertain.

The task of collating these many versions and translations, ranging over more than a thousand years, appearing in Arabic, Latin, German, French, Danish, Swedish, and English, is an undertaking of formidable proportions. Only a person of great erudition and energy would attempt it, and in 1951 such a person did. Per Fraus-Dolus, Professor *emeritus* of Comparative Literature at the University of Oslo, Norway, compiled all the known sources and began the massive task of translation which occupied him until his death in 1957. Portions of his new translation were published in the *Proceedings of the National Museum of Oslo: 1959–*

1960, but they did not arouse much scholarly interest, perhaps because the journal has a limited circulation.

The Fraus-Dolus translation was absolutely literal; in his own introduction to the material, Fraus-Dolus remarked that "it is in the nature of languages that a pretty translation is not accurate, and an accurate translation finds its own beauty without help."

In preparing this full and annotated version of the Fraus-Dolus translation, I have made few alterations. I deleted some repetitive passages; these are indicated in the text. I changed paragraph structure, starting each directly quoted speaker with a new paragraph, according to modern convention. I have omitted the diacritical marks on Arabic names. Finally, I have occasionally altered the original syntax, usually by transposing subordinate clauses so that the meaning is more readily grasped.

THE VIKINGS

Ibn Fadlan's portrait of the Vikings differs markedly from the traditional European view of these people. The first European descriptions of the Vikings were recorded by the clergy; they were the only observers at the time who could write, and they viewed the pagan Northmen with special horror. Here is a typically hyperbolic passage, cited by D. M. Wilson, from a twelfth-century Irish writer:

> In a word, although there were an hundred hard-steeled iron heads on one neck, and an hundred sharp, ready, cool, never rusting, brazen tongues in each head, and an hundred

Introduction

garrulous, loud, unceasing voices from each tongue, they
could not recount or narrate, enumerate or tell, what all the
Irish suffered in common, both men and women, laity and
clergy, old and young, noble and ignoble, of the hardships
and of injuring and of oppression, in every house, from those
valiant, wrathful, purely pagan people.

Modern scholars recognize that such blood-curdling accounts of Viking raids are vastly exaggerated. Yet European
writers still tend to dismiss the Scandinavians as bloody
barbarians, irrelevant to the main flow of Western culture
and ideas. Often this has been done at the expense of a certain
logic. For example, David Talbot Rice writes:

From the eighth to the eleventh centuries indeed the role
of the Vikings was perhaps more influential than that of any
other single ethnic group in Western Europe. . . . The Vikings were thus great travellers and they performed outstand-
ing feats of navigation; their cities were great centres of
trade; their art was original, creative and influential; they
boasted a fine literature and a developed culture. Was it truly
a civilization? It must, I think, be admitted that it was not.
. . . The touch of humanism which is the hallmark of civilization was absent.

This same attitude is reflected in the opinion of Lord
Clark:

When one considers the Icelandic sagas, which are among
the great books of the world, one must admit that the Norsemen produced a culture. But was it civilization? . . . Civilization means something more than energy and will and
creative power: something the early Norsemen hadn't got,

5

but which, even in their time, was beginning to reappear in Western Europe. How can I define it? Well, very shortly, a sense of permanence. The wanderers and invaders were in a continual state of flux. They didn't feel the need to look forward beyond the next March or the next voyage or the next battle. And for that reason it didn't occur to them to build stone houses, or to write books.

The more carefully one reads these views, the more illogical they appear. Indeed, one must wonder why highly educated and intelligent European scholars feel so free to dismiss the Vikings with no more than a passing nod. And why the preoccupation with the semantic question of whether the Vikings had a "civilization"? The situation is explicable only if one recognizes a long-standing European bias, springing from traditional views of European prehistory.

Every Western schoolchild is dutifully taught that the Near East is "the cradle of civilization," and that the first civilizations arose in Egypt and Mesopotamia, nourished by the Nile and the Tigris-Euphrates river basins. From here civilization spread to Crete and Greece, and then to Rome, and eventually to the barbarians of northern Europe.

What these barbarians were doing while they waited for the arrival of civilization was not known; nor was the question often raised. The emphasis lay on the process of dissemination, which the late Gordon Childe summarized as "the irradiation of European barbarism by Oriental civilization." Modern scholars held this view, as did Roman and

Introduction

Greek scholars before them. Geoffrey Bibby says: "The history of northern and eastern Europe is viewed from the West and South, with all the preconceptions of men who considered themselves civilized looking upon men whom they considered barbarians."

From this standpoint, the Scandinavians are obviously the farthest from the source of civilization, and logically the last to acquire it; and therefore they are properly regarded as the last of the barbarians, a nagging thorn in the side of those other European areas trying to absorb the wisdom and civilization of the East.

The trouble is that this traditional view of European prehistory has been largely destroyed in the last fifteen years. The development of accurate carbon-dating techniques has made a mess of the old chronology, which supported the old views of diffusion. It now appears indisputable that Europeans were erecting huge megalithic tombs before the Egyptians built the pyramids; Stonehenge is older than the civilization of Mycenaean Greece; metallurgy in Europe may well precede the development of metalworking skills in Greece and Troy.

The meaning of these discoveries has not yet been sorted out, but it is certainly now impossible to regard the prehistoric Europeans as savages idly awaiting the blessings of Eastern civilization. On the contrary, the Europeans seem to have had organizational skills considerable enough to work massive stones, and they seem also to have had impressive astronomical knowledge to build Stonehenge, the first observatory in the world.

7

Introduction

Thus, the European bias toward the civilized East must be called into question, and indeed the very concept of "European barbarism" requires a fresh look. With this in mind, those barbaric remnants, the Vikings, take on a new significance, and we can reexamine what is known of the Scandinavians of the tenth century.

First we should recognize that "the Vikings" were never a clearly unified group. What the Europeans saw were scattered and individual parties of seafarers who came from a vast geographical area—Scandinavia is larger than Portugal, Spain, and France combined—and who sailed from their individual feudal states for the purpose of trade or piracy or both; the Vikings made little distinction. But that is a tendency shared by many seafarers from the Greeks to the Elizabethans.

In fact, for a people who lacked civilization, who "didn't feel the need to look ... beyond the next battle," the Vikings demonstrate remarkably sustained and purposeful behavior. As proof of widespread trading, Arabic coins appear in Scandinavia as early as A.D. 692. During the next four hundred years, the Viking trader-pirates expanded as far west as Newfoundland, as far south as Sicily and Greece (where they left carvings on the lions of Delos), and as far east as the Ural Mountains of Russia, where their traders linked up with caravans arriving from the silk route to China. The Vikings were not empire builders, and it is popular to say that their influence across this vast area was impermanent. Yet it was sufficiently permanent to lend place-names to many localities in England, while to Russia they gave the very name of the nation itself, from the Norse tribe Rus. As for the more subtle influence of their pagan vigor, relentless energy, and system of values, the manuscript of Ibn Fadlan shows us how many typically Norse attitudes have been retained to the present day. Indeed, there is something strikingly familiar to the modern sensibility about the Viking way of life, and something profoundly appealing.

ABOUT THE AUTHOR

A word should be said about Ibn Fadlan, the man who speaks to us with such a distinctive voice despite the passage of more than a thousand years and the filter of transcribers and translators from a dozen linguistic and cultural traditions.

We know almost nothing of him personally. Apparently he was educated and, from his exploits, he could not have been very old. He states explicitly that he was a familiar of the Caliph, whom he did not particularly admire. (In this he was not alone, for the Caliph al-Muqtadir was twice deposed and finally slain by one of his own officers.)

Of his society, we know more. In the tenth century, Bagdad, the City of Peace, was the most civilized city on earth. More than a million inhabitants lived within its famous circular walls. Bagdad was the focus of intellectual and commercial excitement, within an environment of extraordinary grace, elegance, and splendor. There were perfumed gardens, cool shady arbors, and the accumulated riches of a vast empire.

Introduction

The Arabs of Bagdad were Muslim and fiercely dedicated to that religion. But they were also exposed to peoples who looked, acted, and believed differently from them. The Arabs were, in fact, the least provincial people in the world of that time, and this made them superb observers of foreign cultures.

Ibn Fadlan himself is clearly an intelligent and observant man. He is interested in both the everyday details of life and the beliefs of the people he meets. Much that he witnessed struck him as vulgar, obscene, and barbaric, but he wastes little time in indignation; once he expresses his disapproval, he goes right back to his unblinking observations. And he reports what he sees with remarkably little condescension.

His manner of reporting may seem eccentric to Western sensibilities; he does not tell a story as we are accustomed to hearing one. We tend to forget that our own sense of drama originates in an oral tradition—a live performance by a bard before an audience that must often have been restless and impatient, or else sleepy after a heavy meal. Our oldest stories, the *Iliad, Beowulf,* the *Song of Roland,* were all intended to be sung by singers whose chief function and first obligation was entertainment.

But Ibn Fadlan was a writer, and his principal aim was not entertainment. Nor was it to glorify some listening patron, or to reinforce the myths of the society in which he lived. On the contrary, he was an ambassador delivering a report; his tone is that of a tax auditor, not a bard; an anthropologist, not a dramatist. Indeed, he often slights the most exciting elements of his narrative rather than let them interfere with his clear and level-headed account.

Introduction

At times this dispassion is so irritating we fail to recognize how extraordinary a spectator he really is. For hundreds of years after Ibn Fadlan, the tradition among travelers was to write wildly speculative, fanciful chronicles of foreign marvels—talking animals, feathered men who flew, encounters with behemoths and unicorns. As recently as two hundred years ago, otherwise sober Europeans were filling their journals with nonsense about African baboons that waged war with farmers, and so on.

Ibn Fadlan never speculates. Every word rings true, and whenever he reports by hearsay, he is careful to say so. He is equally careful to specify when he is an eyewitness: that is why he uses the phrase "I saw with my own eyes" over and over.

In the end, it is this quality of absolute truthfulness which makes his tale so horrifying. For his encounter with the monsters of the mist, the "eaters of the dead," is told with the same attention to detail, the same careful skepticism, that marks the other portions of the manuscript.

In any case, the reader may judge for himself.

The departure from the City of Peace

Praise be to God, the Merciful, the Compassionate, the Lord of the Two Worlds, and blessing and peace upon the Prince of Prophets, our Lord and Master Muhammad, whom God bless and preserve with abiding and continuing peace and blessings until the Day of the Faith!

This is the book of Ahmad ibn-Fadlan, ibn-al-Abbas, ibn-Rasid, ibn-Hammad, a client of Muhammad ibn-Sulayman, the ambassador from al-Muqtadir to the King of the Saqaliba, in which he recounts what he saw in the land of the Turks, the Hazars, the Saqaliba, the Baskirs, the Rus, and the Northmen, of the histories of their kings and the way they act in many affairs of their life.

The letter of the Yiltawar, King of the Saqaliba, reached the Commander of the Faithful, al-Muqtadir. He asked him therein to send someone who would instruct him in religion and make him acquainted with the laws of Islam; who would build for him a mosque and erect for him a pulpit from which might be carried out the mission of converting his people in all the districts of his kingdom; and also for advice in the construction of fortifications and defense works. And he prayed the Caliph to do these things. The intermediary in this matter was Dadir al-Hurami.

The Commander of the Faithful, al-Muqtadir, as many know, was not a strong and just caliph, but drawn to pleasures and the flattering speeches of his officers, who played him the fool and jested mightily behind his back. I was not of this company, or especially beloved of the Caliph, for the reason that follows.

In the City of Peace lived an elderly merchant of the name ibn-Qarin, rich in all things but lacking a generous heart and a love of man. He hoarded his gold and likewise his young wife, whom none had ever seen but all bespoke as beautiful beyond imagining. On a certain day, the Caliph sent me to deliver to ibn-Qarin a message, and I presented myself to the house of the merchant and sought entrance therein with my letter and seal. Until today, I do not know the import of the letter, but it does not matter.

The merchant was not at home, being abroad on some business; I explained to the door servant that I must await his return, since the Caliph had instructed I must deliver the message into his hands from mine only. Thus the door servant admitted me into the house, which procedure took some passing of time, for the door to the house had many bolts, locks, bars, and fasteners, as is common in the dwellings of misers. At length I was admitted and I waited all day, growing hungry and thirsty, but was offered no refreshments by the servants of the niggardly merchant.

In the heat of the afternoon, when all about me the house was still and the servants slept, I, too, felt drowsy. Then before me I saw an apparition in white, a woman young and beautiful, whom I took to be the very wife no man had ever seen. She did not speak, but with gestures led me to another room, and there locked the door. I enjoyed her upon the spot, in which matter she required no encouragement, for her husband was old and no doubt neglectful. Thus did the afternoon pass quickly, until we heard the master of the house making his return. Immediately the wife arose and departed, having never uttered a word in my presence, and I was left to arrange my garments in some haste.

Now I should have been apprehended for certain were it not for these same many locks and bolts which impeded the miser's entry into his own home. Even so, the merchant ibn-Qarin found me in the adjoining room, and he viewed me with suspicion, asking why I should be there and not in the courtyard, where it was proper for a messenger to wait. I replied that I was famished and faint, and had searched for food and shade. This was a poor lie and he did not believe it; he complained to the Caliph, who I know was amused in private and yet compelled to adopt a stern face to the public. Thus when the ruler of the Saqaliba asked for a mission from the Caliph, this same spiteful ibn-Qarin urged I be sent, and so I was.

In our company there was the ambassador of the King of Saqaliba who was called Abdallah ibn-Bastu al-Hazari, a tedious and windy man who talked overmuch. There was also Takin al-Turki, Bars al-Saqlabi, both guides on the journey, and I, too. We bore gifts for the ruler, for his wife, his children, and his generals. Also we brought certain drugs, which were given over to the care of Sausan al-Rasi. This was our party.

So we started on Thursday, the 11th of Safar of the year 309 [June 21, 921], from the City of Peace [Bagdad]. We stopped a day in Nahrawan, and from there went swiftly until we reached al-Daskara, where we stopped for three days. Then we traveled straight onward without any detours until we reached Hulwan. There we stayed two days. From there we went to Qirmisin, where we remained two days. Then we started and traveled until we reached Hamadan, where we remained three days. Then we went farther to Sawa, where we remained two days. From there we came to Ray, where we remained eleven days waiting for Ahmad ibn-Ali, the brother of al-Rasi, because he was in Huwar al-Ray. Then we went to Huwar al-Ray and remained there three days.

This passage gives the flavor of Ibn Fadlan's descriptions of travel. Perhaps a quarter of the entire manuscript is written in this fashion, simply listing the names of settlements and the number of days spent at each. Most of this material has been deleted.

Apparently, Ibn Fadlan's party is traveling northward, and eventually they are required to halt for winter.

Our stay in Gurganiya was lengthy; we stayed there some days of the month of Ragab [November] and during the whole of Saban, Ramadan, and Sawwal. Our long stay was brought about by the cold and its bitterness. Verily, they told me that two men took camels into the forests to get wood. They forgot, however, to take flint and tinder with them, and hence slept in the night without a fire. When they got up the next morning, they found the camels had been frozen stiff from the cold.

Verily, I beheld the marketplace and streets of Gurganiya completely deserted because of the cold. One could stroll the streets without meeting anyone. Once as I came out of my bath, I entered my house and looked at my beard, which was a lump of ice. I had to thaw it out before the fire. I lived night and day in a house that was inside another house, in which a Turkish felt tent was pitched, and I myself was wrapped up in many clothes and fur rugs. But in spite of all this, my cheeks often stuck to the pillow at night.

In this extremity of cold, I saw that the earth sometimes forms great cracks, and a large and ancient tree may split into two halves from this.

About the middle of Sawwal of the year 309 [February, 922], the weather began to change, the river thawed, and we got ourselves the necessary things for the journey. We bought Turkish camels and skin boats made out of camel hides, in preparation for the rivers we would have to cross in the land of Turks.

We laid in a supply of bread, millet, and salted meat for three months. Our acquaintances in the town directed us in laying in garments, as much as was needed. They depicted the coming hardships in fearful terms, and we believed they exaggerated the story, yet when we underwent this, it was far greater than what had been told to us.

Each of us put on a jacket, over that a coat, over that a tulup, over that a burka, and a helmet of felt out of which only the two eyes could look. We also had a simple pair of underdrawers with trousers over them, and house shoes and over these another pair of boots. When one of us got on a camel, he could not move because of his clothes.

17

The doctor of the law and the teacher and the pages who traveled with us from Bagdad departed from us now, fearing to enter this new country, so I, the ambassador, his brother-in-law and two pages, Takin and Bars, proceeded.*

The caravan was ready to start. We took into our service a guide from the inhabitants of the town whose name was Qlawus. Then, trusting in the all-powerful and exalted God, we started on Monday, the third of Dulqada of the year 309 [March 3, 922] from the town Gurganiya.

That same day, we stopped at the burg called Zamgan: that is, the gateway to the Turks. The next morning early, we proceeded to Git. There so much snow fell that the camels plunged in it up to their knees; hence we halted two days.

Then we sped straight into the land of the Turks without meeting anyone on the barren and even steppe. We rode ten days in bitter cold and unbroken snowstorms, in comparison with which the cold in Chwarezm seemed like a summer day, so that we forgot all our previous discomforts and were about at the point of giving up.

One day when we underwent the most savage cold weather, Takin the page was riding next to me, and along

---

* Throughout the manuscript, Ibn Fadlan is inexact about the size and composition of his party. Whether this apparent carelessness reflects his assumption that the reader knows the composition of the caravan, or whether it is a consequence of lost passages of the text, one cannot be sure. Social conventions may also be a factor, for Ibn Fadlan never states that his party is greater than a few individuals, when in fact it probably numbered a hundred people or more, and twice as many horses and camels. But Ibn Fadlan does not count—literally—slaves, servants, and lesser members of the caravan.

with him one of the Turks, who was talking to him in Turkish. Takin laughed and said to me, "This Turk says, 'What will our Lord have of us? He is killing us with cold. If we knew what he wanted, we would let him have it.' "

And then I said, "Tell him He only wishes that you say, 'There is no God save Allah.' "

The Turk laughed and answered, "If I knew it, I would say it."

Then we came to a forest where there was a large quantity of dry wood and we halted. The caravan lit fires, we warmed ourselves, took off our clothes, and spread them out to dry.

⎡ Apparently, Ibn Fadlan's party was entering a warmer⎤
⎢ region, because he makes no further reference to extreme⎥
⎣ cold. ⎦

We set out again and rode every day from midnight until the time of the afternoon prayer—hastening more from midday on—and then we halted. When we had ridden fifteen nights in this manner, we arrived at a large mountain with many great rocks. There are springs there that jet out from the rocks and the water stays in pools. From this place, we crossed on until we reached a Turkish tribe, which is called the Oguz.

The ways of the Oguz Turks

The Oguz are nomads and have houses of felt. They stay for a time in one place and then travel on. Their dwellings are placed here and there according to nomadic custom. Although they lead a hard existence, they are like asses gone astray. They have no religious bonds with God. They never pray, but instead call their headmen Lords. When one of them takes counsel with his chief about something, he says, "O Lord, what shall I do in this or that matter?"

Their undertakings are based upon counsel solely among themselves. I have heard them say, "There is no God but Allah and Muhammad is the prophet of Allah," but they speak thus so as to get close to any Muslims, and not because they believe it.

The ruler of the Oguz Turks is called Yabgu. That is the name of the ruler and everyone who rules over this tribe bears the name. His subordinate is always called Kudarkin and so each subordinate to a chieftain is called Kudarkin.

The Oguz do not wash themselves after either defecation or urination, nor do they bathe after ejaculation, or on other occasions. They have nothing whatever to do with water, especially in winter. No merchants or other Muhammadans may perform ablution in their presence except in the night when the Turks do not see it, for they get angry and say, "This man wishes to put a spell on us, for he is immersing himself in water," and they compel him to pay a fine.

None of the Muhammadans can enter Turkish country until one of the Oguz agrees to become his host, with whom he stays and for whom he brings garments from the land of Islam, and for his wife some pepper, millet, raisins, and nuts. When the Muslim comes to his host, the latter pitches a tent for him and brings him sheep, so that the Muslim may himself slaughter the sheep. The Turks never slaughter; they beat the sheep on the head until it is dead.

Oguz women never veil themselves in the presence of their own men or others. Nor does the woman cover any of her bodily parts in the presence of any person. One day we stopped off with a Turk and were seated in his tent. The man's wife was present. As we conversed, the woman uncovered her pudendum and scratched it, and we saw her doing so. We veiled our faces and said, "I beg God's pardon." At this her husband laughed and said to the interpreter, "Tell them we uncover it in your presence so that you may see it and be abashed, but it is not to be attained. This is better than when you cover it up and yet it is attainable."

Adultery is unknown among them. Whomsoever they find to be an adulterer, they tear him in two. This comes about so: they bring together the branches of two trees, tie him to the branches, and then let both trees go so the man who was tied to the trees is torn in two.

Eaters of the Dead

The custom of pederasty is counted by the Turks a terrible sin. There once came a merchant to stay with the clan of the Kudarkin. This merchant stayed with his host for a time to buy sheep. Now, the host had a beardless son, and the guest sought unceasingly to lead him astray until he got the boy to consent to his will. In the meantime, the Turkish host entered and caught them *in flagrante delicto.*

The Turks wished to kill the merchant and also the son for this offense. But after much pleading the merchant was permitted to ransom himself. He paid his host with four hundred sheep for what he had done to his son, and then the merchant hastily departed from the land of the Turks.

All the Turks pluck their beards with the exception of their mustaches.

Their marriage customs are as follows: one of them asks for the hand of a female member of another's family, against such and such a marriage price. The marriage price often consists of camels, pack animals, and other things. No one can take a wife until he has fulfilled the obligation, on which he has come to an understanding with the men of the family. If, however, he has met it, then he comes without any ado, enters the abode where she is, takes her in the presence of her father, mother, and brothers, and they do not prevent him.

If a man dies who has a wife and children, then the eldest of his sons takes her to wife if she is not his mother.

If one of the Turks becomes sick and has slaves, they look after him and no one of his family comes near him. A tent is pitched for him apart from the houses and he does not depart from it until he dies or gets well. If, however, he is a slave or a poor man, they leave him in the desert and go on their way.

When one of their prominent men dies, they dig for him a great pit in the form of a house and they go to him, dress him in a *qurtaq* with his belt and bow, and put a drinking cup of wood with intoxicating drink in his hand. They take his entire possessions and put them in this house. Then they set him down in it also. Then they build another house over him and make a kind of cupola out of mud.

Then they kill his horses. They kill one or two hundred, as many as he has, at the site of the grave. Then they eat the flesh down to the head, the hooves, the hide, and the tail, for they hang these up on wooden poles and say, "These are his steeds on which he rides to Paradise."

If he has been a hero and slain enemies, they carve wooden statues in the number of those whom he has slain, place them upon his grave, and say, "These are his pages who serve him in Paradise."

Sometimes they delay killing the horses for a day or two, and then an old man from among their elderly ones stirs them up by saying, "I have seen the dead man in my sleep and he said to me: 'Here thou seest me. My comrades have overtaken me and my feet were too weak to follow them. I cannot overtake them and so have remained alone.' " In this case, the people slaughter his steeds and hang them up on his grave. After a day or two, the same elder comes to them and says, "I have seen the dead man in a dream and he said: 'Inform my family that I have recovered from my plight.' "

In this way the old man preserves the ways of the Oguz, for there might otherwise be a desire for the living to retain the horses of the dead.*

At length we traveled on in the Turkish kingdom. One morning one of the Turks met us. He was ugly in figure, dirty in appearance, despicable in manner, and base in nature. He said: "Halt." The whole caravan halted in obedience to his command. Then he said, "No single one of you may proceed." We said to him, "We are friends of the Kudarkin." He began to laugh and said, "Who is the Kudarkin? I defecate on his beard."

No man among us knew what to do at these words, but then the Turk said, *"Bekend"*; that is, "bread" in the language of Chwarezm. I gave him a few sheets of bread. He took them and said, "You may go further. I take pity upon you."

We came to the district of the army commander whose name was Etrek ibn-al-Qatagan. He pitched Turkish tents for us and had us stay in them. He himself had a large establishment, servants and large dwellings. He drove in sheep for us that we might slaughter them, and put horses at our disposal for riding. The Turks speak of him as their best

* Farzan, an unabashed admirer of Ibn Fadlan, believes that this paragraph reveals "the sensibility of a modern anthropologist, recording not only the customs of a people, but the mechanisms which act to enforce those customs. The economic meaning of killing a nomad leader's horses is the approximate equivalent of modern death-taxes; that is, it tends to retard the accumulation of inherited wealth in a family. Although demanded by religion, this could not have been a popular practice, any more than it is during the present day. Ibn Fadlan most astutely demonstrates the way it is imposed upon the reluctant."

horseman, and in truth I saw one day, when he raced with us on his horse and as a goose flew over us, he strung his bow and then, guiding his horse under it, shot at the goose and brought it down.

I presented to him a suit from Merv, a pair of boots of red leather, a coat of brocade, and five coats of silk. He accepted these with glowing words of praise. He removed the brocade coat that he wore in order to don the garments of honor I had just given him. Then I saw that the *qurtaq* which he had underneath was fraying apart and filthy, but it is their custom that no one shall remove the garment that he wears next to his body until it disintegrates. Verily also he plucked out his entire beard and even his mustache, so that he looked like a eunuch. And yet, as I have observed, he was their best horseman.

I believed that these fine gifts should win his friendship to us, but such was not to be. He was a treacherous man.

One day he sent for the leaders close to him; that is, Tarhan, Yanal, and Glyz. Tarhan was the most influential among them; he was crippled and blind and had a maimed hand. Then he said to them: "These are the messengers of the King of the Arabs to the chief of the Bulgars, and I should not let them pass without taking counsel with you."

Then Tarhan spoke: "This is a matter that we have never yet seen. Never has the ambassador of the Sultan traveled through our country since we and our ancestors have been here. My feeling is that the Sultan is playing us a trick. These men he really sent to the Hazars to stir them up against us. The best is to hew these ambassadors in twain and we shall take all they have."

Another counselor said: "No, we should rather take what they have and leave them naked so that they may return thither whence they came."

And another said: "No, we have captives with the King of the Hazars, so we ought to send these men to ransom them."

They kept discussing these matters among themselves for seven days, while we were in a situation similar to death, until they agreed to open the road and let us pass. We gave to Tarhan as a garment of honor two caftans from Merv and also pepper, millet, and some sheets of bread.

And we traveled forth until we came to the river Bagindi. There we took our skin boats which had been made from camel hides, spread them out, and loaded the goods from the Turkish camels. When each boat was full, a group of five, six, or four men sat in them. They took birchwood branches in their hands and used them like oars and kept on rowing while the water carried the boat down and spun it around. Finally we got across. With regard to the horses and camels, they came swimming across.

It is absolutely necessary when crossing a river that first of all a group of warriors with weapons should be transported across before any of the caravan, in order that a vanguard be established to prevent attack by Baskirs while the main body is crossing the river.

Thus we crossed the river Bagindi, and then the river called Gam, in the same way. Then the Odil, then the Adrn, then the Wars, then the Ahti, then the Wbna. All these are big rivers.

26

Then we arrived at the Pecenegs. These had encamped by a still lake like the sea. They are dark brown, powerful people and the men shave their beards. They are poor in contrast to the Oguz, for I saw men among the Oguz who possessed 10,000 horses and 100,000 sheep. But the Pecenegs are poor, and we remained only a day with them.

Then we started out and came to the river Gayih. This is the largest, widest, swiftest that we saw. Verily I saw how a skin boat overturned in it, and those on it were drowned. Many of the company perished and a number of the camels and horses were drowned. We crossed this river with difficulty. Then we went a few days farther on and crossed the river Gaha, then the river Azhn, then the Bagag, then the Smur, then the Knal, then the Suh, and then the river Kiglu. At length we arrived in the land of the Baskirs.

> The Yakut manuscript contains a short description of Ibn Fadlan's stay among the Baskirs; many scholars question the authenticity of these passages. The actual descriptions are unusually vague and tedious, consisting chiefly of lists of the chiefs and nobles encountered. Ibn Fadlan himself suggests the Baskirs are not worth bothering with, an uncharacteristic statement from this relentlessly curious traveler.

At length we left the land of the Baskirs, and crossed the river Germsan, the river Urn, the river Urm, then the river Wtig, the river Nbasnh, then the river Gawsin. Between the rivers that we mention, the distance is a journey of two, three, or four days in each case.

Then we came to the land of the Bulgars, which begins at the shore of the river Vclga.

First contact with the Northmen

I saw with my own eyes how the Northmen* had arrived with their wares, and pitched their camp along the Volga. Never did I see a people so gigantic: they are tall as palm trees, and florid and ruddy in complexion. They wear neither camisoles nor caftans, but the men among them wear a garment of rough cloth, which is thrown over one side, so that one hand remains free.

Every Northman carries an axe, a dagger, and a sword, and without these weapons they are never seen. Their swords are broad, with wavy lines, and of Frankish make. From the tip of the fingernails to the neck, each man of them is tattooed with pictures of trees, living beings, and other things.

The women carry, fastened to their breast, a little case of iron, copper, silver, or gold, according to the wealth and resources of their husbands. Fastened to the case they wear

---

* Actually, Ibn Fadlan's word for them here was "Rus," the name of this particular tribe of Northmen. In the text, he sometimes calls the Scandinavians by their particular tribal name, and sometimes he calls them "Varangians" as a generic term. Historians now reserve the term Varangian for the Scandinavian mercenaries employed by the Byzantine Empire. To avoid confusion, in this translation the terms "Northmen" and "Norsemen" are everywhere employed.

28

a ring, and upon that a dagger, all attached to their breast. About their necks they wear gold and silver chains.

They are the filthiest race that God ever created. They do not wipe themselves after going to stool, or wash themselves after a nocturnal pollution, anymore than if they were wild asses.

They come from their own country, anchor their ships in the Volga, which is a great river, and build large wooden houses on its banks. In every such house there live ten or twenty, more or fewer. Each man has a couch, where he sits with the beautiful girls he has for sale. He is as likely as not to enjoy one of them while a friend looks on. At times several of them will be thus engaged at the same moment, each in full view of the others.

Now and again, a merchant will resort to a house to purchase a girl, and find her master thus embracing her, and not giving over until he has fully had his will; in this there is thought nothing remarkable.

Every morning a slave girl comes and brings a tub of water and places it before her master. He proceeds to wash his face and hands, and then his hair, combing it over the vessel. Thereupon he blows his nose, and spits into the tub, and, leaving no dirt behind, conveys it all into this water. When he has finished, the girl carries the tub to the man next to him, who does the same. Thus she continues carrying the tub from one to another, till each of those who are in the house has blown his nose and spit into the tub, and washed his face and hair.

This is the normal way of things among the Northmen,

as I have seen with my own eyes. Yet at the period of our arrival among them, there was some discontent among the giant people, the nature of which was thus:

Their principal chieftain, a man of the name Wyglif, had fallen ill, and was set up in a sick-tent at a distance from the camp, with bread and water. No one approached or spoke to him, or visited him the whole time. No slaves nurtured him, for the Northmen believe that a man must recover from any sickness according to his own strength. Many among them believed that Wyglif would never return to join them in the camp, but instead would die.

Now, one of their number, a young noble called Buliwyf, was chosen to be their new leader, but he was not accepted while the sick chieftain still lived. This was the cause of uneasiness, at the time of our arrival. Yet also there was no aspect of sorrow or weeping among the people encamped on the Volga.

The Northmen place great importance on the duty of the host. They greet every visitor with warmth and hospitality, much food and clothing, and the earls and nobles compete for the honor of the greatest hospitality. The party of our caravan was brought before Buliwyf and a great feast was given us. Over this Buliwyf himself presided, and I saw him to be a tall man, and strong, with skin and hair and beard of pure white. He had the bearing of a leader.

Recognizing the honor of the feast, our party made a show of eating, yet the food was vile and the manner of the feast contained much throwing of food and drink, and great laughing and merriment. It was common in the middle of this rude banquet for an earl to disport with a slave girl in full view of his fellows.

Seeing this, I turned away and said, "I beg God's pardon," and the Northmen laughed much at my discomfiture. One of their number translated for me that they believe God looks favorably upon such open pleasures. He said to me, "You Arabs are like old women, you tremble at the sight of life."

I said in answer, "I am a guest among you, and Allah shall lead me to righteousness."

This was reason for further laughter, but I do not know for what cause they should find a joke.

The custom of the Northmen reveres the life of war. Verily, these huge men fight continually; they are never at peace, neither among themselves nor among different tribes of their kind. They sing songs of their warfare and bravery, and believe that the death of a warrior is the highest honor.

At the banquet of Buliwyf, a member of their kind sang a song of bravery and battle that was much enjoyed, though little attended. The strong drink of the Northmen soon renders them as animals and stray asses; in the midst of the song there was ejaculation and also mortal combat over some intoxicated quarrel of two warriors. The bard did not cease his song through all these events; verily I saw flying blood spatter his face, and yet he wiped it away without a pause in his singing.

This impressed me greatly.

Now it happened that this Buliwyf, who was drunk as the rest, commanded that I should sing a song for them.

He was most insistent. Not wishing to anger him, I recited from the Koran, with the translator repeating my words in their Norse tongue. I was received no better than their own minstrel, and afterward I asked the forgiveness of Allah for the treatment of His holy words, and also for the translation,* which I sensed to be thoughtless, for in truth the translator was himself drunk.

We had stayed two days among the Northmen, and on the morning we planned to leave, we were told by the translator that the chieftain Wyglif had died. I sought to witness what then befell.

First, they laid him in his grave, over which a roof was erected, for the space of ten days,† until they had completed the cutting and sewing of his clothes. They also brought together his goods, and divided them into three parts. The first of these is for his family; the second is expended for the

---

* Arabs have always been uneasy about translating the Koran. The earliest sheiks held that the holy book could not be translated, an injunction apparently based on religious considerations. But everyone who has attempted a translation agrees for the most secular reasons: Arabic is by nature a succinct language, and the Koran is composed as poetry and therefore even more concentrated. The difficulties of conveying literal meaning—to say nothing of the grace and elegance of the original Arabic—have led translators to preface their work with prolonged and abject apologies.

At the same time, Islam is an active, expansive way of thought, and the tenth century was one of its peak periods of dissemination. This expansion inevitably necessitated translations for the use of new converts, and translations were made, but never happily from the standpoint of the Arabs.

† This alone was startling to an Arab observer from a warm climate. Muslim practice called for quick burial, often the same day as the death, after a short ceremony of ritual washing and prayer.

garments they make; and with the third they purchase strong drink, against the day when a girl resigns herself to death, and is burned with her master.

To the use of wine they abandon themselves in mad fashion, drinking it day and night, as I have already said. Not seldom does one die with a cup in his hand.

The family of Wyglif asked of all his girls and pages, "Which of you will die with him?" Then one of them answered, "I." From the time she uttered that word, she was no longer free; should she wish to draw back, she is not permitted.

The girl who so spoke was then committed to two other girls, who were to keep watch over her, accompany her wherever she went, and even, on occasion, wash her feet. The people occupied themselves with the dead man—cutting out the clothes for him, and preparing whatever else was needful. During the whole of this period, the girl gave herself over to drinking and singing, and was cheerful and gay.

During this time, Buliwyf, the noble who would next be king or chieftain, found a rival whose name was Thorkel. Him I did not know, but he was ugly and foul, a dark man among this ruddy fair race. He plotted to be chieftain himself. All this I learned from the translator, for there was no outward sign in the funeral preparations that anything was not according to custom.

Buliwyf himself did not direct the preparations, for he was not the family of Wyglif, and it is the rule that the family prepares for the funeral. Buliwyf joined the general merriment and celebration, and acted no part of kingly conduct, except during the banquets of the night, when he sat in the high seat that was reserved to the king.

This was the manner of his sitting: when a Northman is truly king, he sits at the head of the table in a large stone chair with stone arms. Such was the chair of Wyglif, but Buliwyf did not sit in it as a normal man would sit. Instead he sat upon one arm, a position from which he fell when he drank overmuch, or laughed with great excess. It was the custom that he could not sit in the chair until Wyglif was buried.

All this time, Thorkel plotted and conferred among the other earls. I came to know that I was suspected as some sorcerer or witch, which distressed me much. The translator, who did not believe these tales, told me that Thorkel said I had caused Wyglif to die, and had caused Buliwyf to be the next chief; yet verily I had no part in any of this.

After some days, I sought to leave with my party of ibn-Bastu and Takin and Bars, and yet the Northmen would not permit us to leave, saying that we must stay to the funeral, and threatening us with their daggers, which they always carried. Thus we stayed.

When the day was come that Wyglif and the girl were to be committed to the flames, his ship was drawn ashore on the banks of the river. Four corner blocks of birch and other woods had been positioned around it; also large wooden figures in the semblance of human beings.

In the meantime the people began to walk to and fro, uttering words that I did not understand. The language of the Northmen is ugly to the ear and difficult to comprehend.

The dead chief, meanwhile, lay at a distance in his grave, from which they had not yet removed him. Next they brought a couch, placed it in the ship, and covered it with Greek cloth of gold, and pillows of the same material. There then came an old crone, whom they call the angel of death, and she spread the personal articles on the couch. It was she who attended to the sewing of the garments, and to all the equipment. It was she, also, who was to slay the girl. I saw the crone with my own eyes. She was dark, thickset, with a lowering countenance.

When they came to the grave, they removed the roof and drew out the dead man. Then I saw that he had turned quite black, by reason of the coldness of that country. Near him in the grave they had placed strong drink, fruits, and a lute; and these they now took out. Except for his color, the dead man Wyglif had not changed.

Now I saw Buliwyf and Thorkel standing side by side, making a great show of friendship during the burial ceremony, and yet it was apparent that there was no truth to their appearances.

The dead king Wyglif was now clothed in drawers, leggings, boots, and a caftan of gold cloth, and on his head was placed a cap made of gold cloth, trimmed in sable. Then he was carried to a tent in the ship; they seated him on a quilted couch, supported him with pillows, and brought strong drink, fruits, and basil, which they placed alongside him.

Then they brought a dog, which they cut in two, and threw into the ship. They laid all his weapons beside him, and led up two horses, which they chased until they were dripping with sweat, whereupon Buliwyf killed one with his sword and Thorkel killed the second, cutting them into pieces with their swords and flinging the pieces forth into the ship. Buliwyf killed his horse less swiftly, which seemed to have some import to those who watched, but I did not know the meaning.

Two oxen were then brought forward, cut into pieces, and flung into the ship. Finally they brought a cock and a hen, killed them, and threw them in also.

The girl who had devoted herself to death meanwhile walked to and fro, entering one after another of the tents that they had there. The occupant of each tent lay with her, saying, "Tell your master I did this only for love of him."

Now it was late in the afternoon. They led the girl to an object they had constructed, which looked like the frame of a door. She placed her feet on the extended hands of the men, who raised her above the framework. She uttered something in her language, whereupon they let her down. Then again they raised her, and she did as before. Once more they let her down, and then lifted her a third time. Then they handed her a hen, whose head she cut off and threw away.

I inquired of the interpreter what it was she had done. He replied: "The first time she said, 'Lo, I see here my father and mother'; the second time, 'Lo, now I see all my deceased relatives sitting'; the third time, 'Lo, there is my master, who is sitting in Paradise. Paradise is so beautiful, so green. With him are his men and boys. He calls me, so bring me to him.'"

Then they led her away to the ship. Here she took off her two bracelets and gave them to the old woman who was called the angel of death, and who was to murder her. She also drew off her two anklets, and passed them to the two serving maids, who were the daughters of the angel of death. Then they lifted her into the ship, but did not yet admit her to the tent.

Now men came up with shields and staves, and handed her a cup of strong drink. This she took, sang over it, and emptied it. The interpreter told me she said, "With this, I take leave of those who are dear to me." Then another cup was handed to her, which she also took, and began a lengthy song. The crone admonished her to drain the cup without lingering, and to enter the tent where her master lay.

By this time, it seemed to me the girl had become dazed.* She made as though she would enter the tent, when suddenly the hag seized her by the head and dragged her in. At this moment the men began to beat upon their shields with the staves, in order to drown the noise of her outcries, which might have terrified the other girls and deterred them from seeking death with their masters in the future.

Six men followed her into the tent, and each and every one of them had carnal companionship with her. Then they laid her down by her master's side, while two of the men seized her feet, and two the hands. The old woman known as the angel of death now knotted a rope around her neck, and handed the ends to two of the men to pull. Then, with a broad-bladed dagger, she smote her between the ribs, and

* Or, possibly, "crazed." The Latin manuscripts read *cerritus*, but the Arabic of Yakut says ر ـ ـ ب , "dazed" or "dazzled."

37

drew the blade forth, while the two men strangled her with the rope till she died.

The kin of the dead Wyglif now drew near and, taking a piece of lighted wood, walked backward naked toward the ship and ignited the ship without ever looking at it. The funeral pyre was soon aflame, and the ship, the tent, the man and the girl, and everything else blew up in a blazing storm of fire.

At my side, one of the Northmen made some comment to the interpreter. I asked the interpreter what was said, and received this answer. "You Arabs," he said, "must be a stupid lot. You take your most beloved and revered man and cast him into the ground to be devoured by creeping things and worms. We, on the other hand, burn him in a twinkling, so that instantly, without a moment's delay, he enters into Paradise."

And in truth, before an hour had passed, ship, wood, and girl had, with the man, turned to ashes.

The aftermath of
the Northmen's funeral

These Scandinavians find no cause for grief in any man's death. A poor man or a slave is a matter of indifference to them, and even a chieftain will provoke no sadness or tears. On the same evening of the funeral of the chief called Wyglif, there was a great feasting in the halls of the Northmen encampment.

Yet I perceived that all was not fitting among these barbarians. I sought counsel with my interpreter. He responded thusly: "It is the plan of Thorkel to see you die, and then to banish Buliwyf. Thorkel has gathered the support of some earls to himself, but there is dispute in every house and every quarter."

Much distressed, I said, "I have no part in this affair. How shall I act?"

The interpreter said I should flee if I could, but if I were caught, this would be proof of my guilt and I would be treated as a thief. A thief is treated in this fashion: the Northmen lead him to a thick tree, fasten a strong rope about him, string him up, and let him hang until he rots to pieces by the action of the wind and the rain.

Remembering also that I had barely escaped death at the

hands of ibn-al-Qatagan, I chose to act as I had before; that is, I remained among the Northmen until I should be given free passage to continue on my journey.

I inquired of the interpreter whether I should bear gifts to Buliwyf, and also to Thorkel, to favor my departure. He said that I could not bear gifts to both, and that the matter was undecided who would be the new chieftain. Then he said it would be clear in one day and night, and no longer.

For it is true among these Northmen that they have no established way of choosing a new chief when the old leader dies. Strength of arms counts high, but also allegiances of the warriors and the earls and noblemen. In some cases there is no clear successor to the rule, and this was one of such eventualities. My interpreter said that I should bide my time, and also pray. This I did.

Then there came a great storm on the banks of the river Volga, a storm that persisted two days, with driving rain and forceful winds, and after this storm a cold mist lay on the ground. It was thick and white, and a man could not see past a dozen paces.

Now, these same giant Northmen warriors, who by virtue of their enormity and strength of arms and cruel disposition, have nothing to fear in all the world, yet these men fear the mist or fog that comes with storms.

The men of their race are at some pains to conceal their fear, even one from another; the warriors laugh and joke overmuch, and make unreasonable display of carefree emotion. Thus do they prove the reverse; and in truth, their attempt of disguise is childish, so plainly do they pretend not to see the truth, yet verily, each and all of them, throughout their encampment, are making prayers and sacrifices of hens and cocks, and if a man is asked the reason of the sacrifice, he will say, "I make sacrifice for the safety of my faraway family"; or he will say, "I make sacrifice for the success of my trading"; or he will say, "I make sacrifice in honor of such or another deceased member of my family"; or he will say many another reason, and then he will add, "And also for the lifting of the mist."

Now, I accounted it strange for such strong and warlike people to be so fearful of anything as to pretend a lack of fear; and of all the sensible reasons for fear, mist or fog seemed to my way of thinking very greatly inexplicable.

I said to my interpreter that a man could fear wind, or blasting storms of sand, or water floods, or heaving of the ground, or thunder and lightning within the sky, for all of these could injure a man, or kill him, or ruin his dwelling. Yet I said that fog, or mist, contained no threat of harm; in truth it was the least of any form of changing elements.

The interpreter answered to me that I was lacking the beliefs of a sailor. He said that many Arab sailors agreed with the Northmen, in the matter of uneasiness* within the wrapping of mist; so, also, he said all seafarers are made anxious of any mist or fog, because such a condition increases the peril of travel upon the waters.

I said this was sensible, but that when the mist lay upon the land and not the water, I did not understand the reason for any fear. To this the interpreter replied, "The fog is al-

* Interestingly, in both Arabic and Latin, literally "disease."

ways feared, whenever it comes." And he said that it made no difference, on land or water, according to the Northman view.

And then he said to me the Northmen did not, truly, much fear the mist. Also the interpreter said that he, as a man, did not fear the mist. He said that it was only a minor matter, of slight consequence. He said, "It is as a minor ache inside a limb joint, which may come with fog, but no more important."

By this I saw that my interpreter, among the others, denied all manner of concern for the fog, and feigned indifference.

Now it happened that the mist did not lift, although it abated and became thin in the afterpart of the day; the sun appeared as a circle in the sky, but also it was so weak that I could look directly to its light.

In this same day there arrived a Northman boat, containing a noble of their own race. He was a young man with a thin beard, and he traveled with only a small party of pages and slaves, and no women among them. Thus I believed he was no trader, for in this area the Northmen principally sell women.

This same visitor beached his boat, and remained standing with it until nightfall, and no man came near to him, or greeted him, although he was a stranger and in plain sight to all. My interpreter said: "He is a kin of Buliwyf, and will be received at the night banquet."

I said, "Why does he stay at his ship?"

"Because of the mist," answered the interpreter. "It is the custom he must stand in view for many hours, so all can see him and know he is no enemy coming from the mist." This the interpreter said to me with much hesitation.

At the night banquet, I saw the young man come into the hall. Here was he warmly greeted and with much display of surprise; and in this most especially by Buliwyf, who acted as if the young man had just arrived, and had not been standing by his ship many hours. After the several greetings, the youth spoke a passionate speech, which Buliwyf attended with unusual interest: he did not drink and dally with the slave girls, but instead in silence heard the youth, who spoke in a high and cracking voice. At the finish of the tale, the youth seemed about to have tears, and was given a cup of drink.

I inquired of my interpreter what was said. Here was the reply: "He is Wulfgar, and he is the son of Rothgar, a great king in the North. He is kin of Buliwyf and seeks his aid and support on a hero's mission. Wulfgar says the far country suffers a dread and nameless terror, which all the peoples are powerless to oppose, and he asks Buliwyf to make haste to return to the far country and save his people and the kingdom of his father, Rothgar."

I inquired of the interpreter the nature of this terror. He said to me, "It has no name which I can tell."* The inter-

---

* The perils of translation are demonstrated in this sentence. The original Arabic of Yakut reads 'لا مَعْنـى كَلِـمة أَنْ أَحَـدَ رَ أَتَكَلَّـم' and means literally "There is no name I can speak." The Xymos manuscript employs the Latin verb *dare*, with the meaning "I cannot give it a name," implying that the interpreter does not know the correct word in a non-Norse tongue. The Razi manuscript, which also contains the interpreter's speeches in fuller detail, uses the word *edere,*

preter seemed much disturbed by Wulfgar's words, and so also were many of the other Northmen. I saw on the countenance of Buliwyf a dark and gloomy expression. I inquired of the interpreter details of the menace.

The interpreter said to me: "The name cannot be said, for it is forbidden to speak it, lest the utterance of the name call forth the demons." And as he spoke I saw that he was fearful just to think upon these matters, and his pallor was marked, and so I ended my inquiry.

Buliwyf, sitting at the high stone throne, was silent. Verily the assembled earls and vassals and all the slaves and servants were silent, also. No man in the hall spoke. The messenger Wulfgar stood before the company with his head bowed. Never had I seen the merry and rambunctious North people so subdued.

Then into the hall entered the old crone called the angel of death, and she sat beside Buliwyf. From a hide bag she withdrew some bones—whether human or animal I do not know—and these bones she cast upon the ground, speaking low utterances, and she passed her hand over them.

The bones were gathered up, and cast again, and the process repeated with more incantations. Now again was the casting done, and finally she spoke to Buliwyf.

I asked the interpreter the meaning of her speech, but he did not attend me.

---

with the meaning "There is no name that I can make known [to you]." This is the more correct translation. The Northman is literally afraid to say the word, lest it call up demons. In Latin, *edere* has the sense of "giving birth to" and "calling up," as well as its literal meaning, "to put forth." Later paragraphs confirm this sense of the meaning.

Then Buliwyf stood and raised his cup of strong drink, and called to the assembled earls and warriors, making a speech of some good length. One by one, several warriors stood at their places to face him. Not all stood; I counted eleven, and Buliwyf pronounced himself satisfied with this.

Now also I saw that Thorkel appeared much pleased by the proceedings and assumed a more kingly bearing, while Buliwyf paid him no heed, or showed any hatred of him, or even any interest, although they were formerly enemies a few minutes past.

Then the angel of death, this same crone, pointed to me and made some utterance, and then she departed the hall. Now at last my interpreter spoke, and he said: "Buliwyf is called by the gods to leave this place and swiftly, putting behind him all his cares and concerns, to act as a hero to repel the menace of the North. This is fitting, and he must also take eleven warriors with him. And so, also, must he take you."

I said that I was on a mission to the Bulgars, and must follow the instructions of my Caliph, with no delay.

"The angel of death has spoken," my interpreter said. "The party of Buliwyf must be thirteen, and of these one must be no Northman, and so you shall be the thirteenth."

I protested I was not a warrior. Verily I made all the excuses and pleadings that I could imagine might have effect upon this rude company of beings. I demanded that the interpreter convey my words to Buliwyf, and yet he turned away and left the hall, saying this last speech: "Prepare yourself as you think best. You shall leave on the morning light."

45

The journey to
the far country

In this manner was I prevented from continuing my travels to the kingdom of the Yiltawar, King of the Saqaliba, and thus was I unable to discharge the trust of al-Muqtadir, Commander of the Faithful and Caliph of the City of Peace. I gave such instructions as I could to Dadir al-Hurami, and also to the ambassador, Abdallah ibn-Bastu al-Hazari, and also to the pages Takin and Bars. Then I took my leave of them, and how they fared further I never knew.

For myself, I counted my condition no different from a dead man. I was on board one of the Northman vessels, and sailing up the Volga river, northward, with twelve of their company. The others were named thus:

Buliwyf, the chief; his lieutenant or captain, Ecthgow; his earls and nobles, Higlak, Skeld, Weath, Roneth, Halga; his warriors and brave fighters, Helfdane, Edgtho, Rethel, Haltaf, and Herger.* And also I was among them, unable to

* Wulfgar was left behind. Jensen states the Northmen commonly held a messenger as hostage, and this is why "appropriate messengers were the sons of kings, or high nobles, or other persons who had some value to their own community, thus making them fitting hostages." Olaf Jorgensen argues that Wulfgar remained behind because he was afraid to go back.

46

speak their language or to understand their ways, for my interpreter had been left behind. It was only happenstance and the grace of Allah that one of their warriors, Herger, should be a man of parts and knowing some of the Latin tongue. Thus I could understand from Herger what meant the events that transpired. Herger was a young warrior, and very merry; he seemed to find jest in everything, and especially in my own gloom at the departure.

These Northmen are by their own accounting the best sailors in the world, and I saw much love of the oceans and waters in their demeanor. Of the ship there is this: it was as long as twenty-five paces, and as broad as eight and a little more than that, and of excellent construction, of oak wood. Its color was black at every place. It was fitted with a square sail of cloth and trimmed with sealskin ropes.* The helmsman stood upon a small platform near the stern and worked a rudder attached to the side of the vessel in the Roman fashion. The ship was fitted with benches for oars, but never were the oars employed; rather we progressed by sailing alone. At the head of the ship was the wooden carving of a fierce sea monster, such as appears on some Northman vessels; also there was a tail at the stern. In water this ship was stable and quite pleasant for traveling, and the confidence of the warriors elevated my spirits.

Near the helmsman was a bed of skins arranged upon a

---

* Some early authors apparently thought this meant that the sail was hemmed in rope; there are eighteenth-century drawings that show the Viking sails with rope borderings. There is no evidence that this was the case; Ibn Fadlan meant that the sails were trimmed in the nautical sense; i.e., angled to best catch the wind, by the use of sealskin ropes as halyards.

network of ropes, with a skin covering. This was the bed of Buliwyf; the other warriors slept upon the deck here and there, wrapping skins about them, and I did as much also.

We traveled upon the river for three days, passing many small settlements at the edge of the water. At none of these did we stop. Then we came upon a large encampment in a bend in the river Volga. Here were many hundreds of peoples, and a town of good size, and in the center of the town a kremlin, or fortress, with earthen walls and all of impressive dimensions. I asked Herger what was this place.

Herger said to me, "This is the city of Bulgar, of the kingdom of the Saqaliba. That is the kremlin of the Yiltawar, King of the Saqaliba."

I replied, "This is the very King I was sent to see as emissary from my Caliph," and with many entreaties I requested to be put upon the shore to do the mission of my Caliph; also I demanded, and made a show of anger, to the extent that I dared.

Verily the Northmen paid me no heed. Herger would not reply to my requests and demands, and finally he laughed into my face, and turned his attention to the sailing of the ship. Thus the Northman's vessel sailed past the city of Bulgar, so close upon the shore that I heard the shouts of merchants and the bleating of sheep, and yet I was helpless and could do no thing, save witness the sight with my eyes. After the passing of an hour even this was refused me, for the Bulgar city is at the bend of the river, as I have said, and soon absent from my view. Thus did I enter and leave Bulgaria.

> The reader may now be hopelessly confused about the geography. Modern Bulgaria is one of the Balkan states; it is bordered by Greece, Yugoslavia, Rumania, and Turkey. But from the ninth to the fifteenth centuries there was another Bulgaria, on the banks of the Volga, roughly 600 miles east of modern Moscow, and this is where Ibn Fadlan was heading. Bulgaria on the Volga was a loose-knit kingdom of some importance, and its capital city, Bulgar, was famous and rich when the Mongols occupied it in A.D. 1237. It is generally believed that Volga Bulgaria and Balkan Bulgaria were populated by related groups of immigrants moving out from the region around the Black Sea during the period A.D. 400–600, but little of substance is known. The old city of Bulgar is in the region of modern Kazan.

Then passed eight more days upon the vessel, still traveling the Volga River, and the land was more mountainous about the valley of the river. Now we came to another branching of the river, where it is called by the Northmen the Oker River, and here we took the leftmost branch and continued on for ten days farther. The air was chill and the wind strong, and much snow lay still upon the ground. They have many great forests also in this region, which the Northmen call Vada.

Then we came to a camp of North people which was Massborg. This was hardly a town but a camp of a few wooden houses, built large in the North fashion; and this town lives by sale of foodstuff to traders who come back and forth along this route. At Massborg we left our vessel, and traveled overland by horse for eighteen days. This was a difficult mountain region, and exceedingly cold, and I was much exhausted by the rigors of the journey. These North people never travel at night. Nor do they often sail at night, but prefer every evening to beach their ship and await the light of dawn before continuing farther.

Yet this was the occurrence: during our travels, the period of the night became so short you could not cook a pot of meat in the time of it. Verily it seemed that as soon as I lay down to sleep I was awakened by the Northmen who said, "Come, it is day, we must continue the journey." Nor was the sleep refreshing in these cold places.

Also, Herger explained to me that in this North country the day is long in the summer, and the night is long in the winter, and rarely are they equal. Then he said to me I should watch in the night for the sky curtain; and upon one evening I did, and I saw in the sky shimmering pale lights, of green and yellow and sometimes blue, which hung as a curtain in the high air. I was much amazed by the sight of this sky curtain but the Northmen count it nothing strange.

Now we traveled for five days down from the mountains, into a region of forests. The forests of the Northlands are cold and dense with gigantic trees. It is a wet and chilling land, in some locations so green that the eyes ache from the brightness of the color; yet in other locations it is black and dark and menacing.

Now we traveled seven days farther, through the forests, and we experienced much rain. Often it is the nature of this rain that it falls with such thickness as to be oppressive; upon one time or another I thought I might drown, so much was the very air filled with water. At other periods, when the wind blew the rain, it was as a sandstorm, stinging the flesh and burning the eyes, and blinding the vision.

[
   Coming from a desert region, Ibn Fadlan would naturally be impressed by the lush green colors, and the abundant rainfall.
]

These Northmen feared no robbers in the forests, and whether from their own great strength or the lack of any bandits, in truth we saw no one in the forests. The North country has few people of any sort, or so it appeared during my sojourn there. We often traveled seven days, or ten, without viewing any settlement or farm or dwelling.

The manner of our journey was this: in the morning we arose, and lacking any ablutions, mounted upon our horses and rode until the middle of the day. Then one or another of the warriors would hunt some game, a small animal or a bird. If it was raining, this food would be consumed without cooking. It rained many days, and in the first instance I chose not to eat the raw flesh, which also was not *dabah* [ritually slaughtered], but after a period I also ate, saying quietly "in the name of God" under my breath, and trusting to God that my predicament should be understood. If it was not raining, a fire was lit with a small ember that was carried with the party, and the food cooked. Also we ate berries and grasses, the names of which I do not know. Then we traveled for the afterpart of each day, which was considerable, until the coming of night, when again we rested, and ate.

Many times at night it rained, and we sought shelter beneath large trees, yet we arose drenched, and our sleeping skins drenched likewise. The Northmen did not grumble at this, for they are cheerful at all times; I alone grumbled, and mightily. They paid me no attention.

Finally I said to Herger, "The rain is cold." To this he laughed. "How can the rain be cold?" he said. "You are cold and you are unhappy. The rain is not cold or unhappy."

I saw that he believed this foolishness, and truly thought me foolish to think otherwise, and yet I did.

Now it happened that one night, while we ate, I said over my food "in the name of God," and Buliwyf inquired of Herger what it was I said. I told to Herger that I believed food must be consecrated, and so I did this according to my beliefs. Buliwyf said to me, "This is the way of the Arabs?" Herger was the translator.

I made this reply: "No, for in truth he who kills the food must make the consecration. I speak the words so as to be not forgetful."*

This the Northmen found a reason of humor. They laughed heartily. Then Buliwyf said to me, "Can you draw sounds?" I did not comprehend his meaning, and inquired of Herger, and there was some talking back and forth, and

---

* This is a typically Muslim sentiment. Unlike Christianity, a religion which in many ways it resembles, Islam does not emphasize a concept of original sin arising from the fall of man. Sin for a Muslim is forgetfulness in carrying out the prescribed daily rituals of the religion. As a corollary, it is a more serious offense to forget the ritual entirely than to remember the ritual and yet fail to carry it out either through extenuating circumstances or personal inadequacy. Thus Ibn Fadlan is saying, in effect, that he is mindful of proper conduct even though he is not acting according to it; this is better than nothing.

finally I understood he meant writing. The Northmen call the speech of Arabs noise or sound. I replied to Buliwyf that I could write, and also read.

He said that I should write for him upon the ground. In the light of the evening fire, I took a stick and wrote, "Praise be to God." All the Northmen looked at the writing. I was commanded to speak what it said, and this I did. Now Buliwyf stared at the writing for a long period, his head sunk upon his chest.

Herger said to me, "Which God do you praise?" I answered that I praised the one God whose name was Allah.

Herger said, "One God cannot be enough."

Now we traveled another day, and passed another night, and then another day. And on the next evening, Buliwyf took a stick and drew in the earth what I had formerly drawn, and commanded me to read.

I spoke aloud the words: "Praise be to God." At this, Buliwyf was satisfied, and I saw that he had contrived a test of me, placing in his memory the symbols I had drawn, to show them to me again.

Now Ecthgow, the lieutenant or captain of Buliwyf, and a warrior less merry than the others, a stern man, spoke to me through the interpreter, Herger. Herger said, "Ecthgow wishes to know if you can draw the sound of his name."

I said that I could, and I took up the stick, and began to draw in the dirt. At once Ecthgow leapt up, flung away the stick, and stamped out my writing. He spoke angry words.

Herger said to me, "Ecthgow does not wish you to draw his name at any time, and this you must promise."

Here I was perplexed, and I saw that Ecthgow was angry with me in the extreme. So also were the others staring at me with concern and anger. I promised to Herger that I would not draw the name of Ecthgow, or of any of the others. At this they were all relieved.

After this, no more was my writing discussed, but Buliwyf gave certain instructions, and whenever it rained I was always directed to the largest tree, and I was given more food than before.

Not always did we sleep in the forests, nor did we always ride through the forests. At the border of some forests, Buliwyf and his warriors would plunge forward, riding at a gallop through the dense trees, without a care or a thought of fear. And then again, at other forests he would draw up and pause, and the warriors would dismount and burn a fire and make some offering of food or a few sheets of hard bread, or a kerchief of cloth, before continuing farther. And then they would ride around the edge of the forest, never entering its depths.

I inquired of Herger why this should be. He said that some forests were safe and some were not, but did not explain further. I asked him, "What is not safe in the forests that are judged so?"

He made this reply: "There are things that no man can conquer, and no sword can kill, and no fire can burn, and such things are in the forests."

I said, "How is this known to be?"

At this he laughed and said, "You Arabs always wish to have reasons for everything. Your hearts are a great bursting bag of reasons."

I said, "And you do not care for reasons?"

"It avails you nothing. We say: A man should be moderately wise, but not overwise, lest he know his fate in advance. The man whose mind is most free of care does not know his fate in advance."

Now, I saw that I must be content with his answer. For it was true that upon one occasion or another, I would make some manner of inquiry, and Herger would reply, and if I did not comprehend his answer, I would ask further, and he would reply further. Yet again, when I made of him an inquiry, he would reply in short fashion, as if the inquiry were of no substance. And then I would have nothing further from him, save a shaking of his head.

Now we continued on. Verily, I can say that some of the forests in the wild North country do provoke a feeling of fear, for which I cannot account. At night, sitting about the fire, the Northmen told stories of dragons and fierce beasts, and also of their ancestors who had slain these creatures. These, they said, were the source of my fear. But they told the stories with no show of fear, and of such beasts, I saw nothing with my own eyes.

One night I heard a grumbling that I took to be thunder, but they said it was the growl of a dragon in the forest. I do not know what is the truth, and report now only what was said to me.

The North country is cold and wet and the sun is seldom seen, for the sky is gray with thick clouds all the day. The people of this region are pale as linen, and their hair is very fair. After so many days of travel, I saw no dark people at all, and indeed I was marveled at by the inhabitants of that

55

region on account of my skin and dark hair. Many times a
farmer or his wife or daughter would come forth to touch
me with a stroking motion; Herger laughed and said they
were trying to brush away the color, thinking it to be painted
upon my flesh. They are ignorant people with no knowledge
of the wideness of the world. Many times they feared me,
and would not approach me close. At one place, I do not
know the name, a child cried out in terror and ran to cling
to his mother when he saw me.

At this, the warriors of Buliwyf laughed with great merriment. But now I observed this thing: with the passing of the
days, the warriors of Buliwyf ceased to laugh, and fell into
an ill humor, more each day. Herger said to me they were
thinking of drink, of which we had been deprived for many
days.

At each farm or dwelling, Buliwyf and his warriors asked
for drink, but in these poor places there was often no liquor,
and they were sorely disappointed, until at last there was no
trace of cheerfulness about them.

At length we arrived at a village, and there the warriors
found drink, and all of the Northmen became intoxicated
in a moment, drinking in raucous fashion, heedless that the
liquor poured over their chins and clothing in their haste.
In truth, one of the company, the solemn warrior Ecthgow,
was so demented from liquor that he was drunk while still
upon his horse, and fell attempting to dismount. Now the
horse kicked him in the head, and I feared for his safety,
but Ecthgow laughed and kicked the horse back.

We remained in this village the space of two days. I was

much amazed, for previously the warriors had shown great haste and purpose in their journey, yet all was now abandoned to drink and stuporous slumber. Then upon the third day, Buliwyf directed that we should continue, and the warriors proceeded, I among them, and they accounted the loss of two days nothing strange.

How many days further we traveled I am not certain. I know that five times we changed horses for fresh mounts, paying for these in the villages with gold and with the little green shells that the Northmen value more highly than any other objects in the world. And at length we came to a village of the name Lenneborg, situated by the sea. The sea was gray, and likewise the sky, and the air was cold and bitter. Here we took another vessel.

This ship was in appearance similar to the one previous, but larger. It was called by the Northmen *Hosbokun,* which means "sea goat," for the reason that the ship bucks the waves as a goat bucks. And also for the reason that the vessel was swift, for among these people the goat is the animal that means swiftness to them.

I was afraid to go upon this sea, for the water was rough and very cold; a man's hand plunged into that sea would lack all feeling in an instant, it was so dire cold. And yet the Northmen were cheerful, and joked and drank for an evening in this sea village of Lenneborg, and disported themselves with many of the women and slave girls. This, I was told, is the Northmen's custom before a sea voyage, for no man knows if he shall survive the journey, and thus he departs with excessive revelry.

In every place we were greeted with great hospitality, for that is considered a virtue by these people. The poorest farmer would set all he had before us, and this without fear that we would kill or rob him, but only out of goodness and grace. The Northmen, I learned, do not countenance robbers or killers of their own race, and treat such men harshly. These beliefs they hold despite the truth of the matter, which is that they are always drunk and brawling like unreasoning animals, and killing each other in hot duels. Yet they do not see this as murder, and any man who murders will be himself killed.

In the same way, they treat their slaves with much kindness, which was a wonder to me.* If a slave turns ill, or dies in some mishap, it is not counted any great loss; and women who are slaves must be ready at any time for the ministrations of any man, in public or in private, day or night. There is no affection for the slaves, and yet there is no brutality for them, either, and they are always fed and clothed by their masters.

Further I learned this: that any man may enjoy a slave, but that the wife of the lowest farmer is respected by the chiefs and earls of the Northmen, as they respect the wives of each other. To force attention on a freeborn woman who is not a slave is a crime, and I was told that a man would be hanged for it, although I never saw this.

* Other eyewitness accounts disagree with Ibn Fadlan's description of the treatment of slaves and adultery, and therefore some authorities question his reliability as a social observer. In fact there was probably substantial local variation, from tribe to tribe, in the accepted treatment of slaves and unfaithful wives.

Chastity among women is said to be a great virtue, but seldom did I see it practiced, for adultery is not accounted as any great matter, and if the wife of any man, low or high, is lusty, the outcome is not thought remarkable. These people are very free in such matters, and the men of the North say that women are devious and cannot be trusted; to this they appear resigned, and speak of it with their usual cheerful demeanor.

I inquired of Herger if he was married, and he said that he had a wife. I inquired with all discretion if she were chaste, and he laughed in my face and said to me: "I sail upon the seas, and I may never return, or I may be absent many years. My wife is not dead." From this, I took the meaning that she was unfaithful to him, and he did not care.

The Northmen do not consider any offspring a bastard if the mother be a wife. The children of slaves are slaves sometimes, and free sometimes; how this is decided I do not know.

In some regions, slaves are marked by a crop of the ear. In other regions, slaves wear a neckband of iron to signify their place. In other regions, slaves have no markings, for that is the local custom.

Pederasty is not known among the Northmen, although they say that other peoples practice it; they themselves claim no interest in the matter, and since it does not occur among them, they have no punishment for it.

All this and more I learned from my talking with Herger, and from witnessing the travels of our party. Further I saw that in each place where we rested the people inquired of

Buliwyf what quest he had undertaken, and when they were informed of its nature—that which I did not yet comprehend—he and his warriors, and I among them, were accorded the highest respect, receiving their prayers and sacrifices and tokens of good wishes.

At sea, as I have said, the Northmen become happy and jubliant, although the ocean was rough and forbidding to my way of thinking, and also to my stomach, which felt most delicate and unsettled. Indeed I purged myself, and then asked Herger why his companions were so happy.

Herger said, "It is because we shall soon be at the home of Buliwyf, the place known as Yatlam, where live his father and his mother and all his relatives, and he has not seen them for many long years."

To this I said, "Are we not going to Wulfgar's land?"

Herger replied, "Yes, but it is fitting that Buliwyf must pay homage to his father and also to his mother."

I saw by their faces that all the other earls, nobles, and warriors were happy as Buliwyf himself. I asked Herger why this was so.

"Buliwyf is our chief, and we are happy for him, and for the power that he will soon have."

I inquired what was this power of which he spoke. "The power of Runding," Herger answered me. "What power is that?" I inquired, to which he made this reply: "The power of the ancients, the power of the giants."

The Northmen believe that in ages past the world was populated by a race of giant men, who have since vanished. The Northmen do not count themselves the descendants of these giants, but they have received some of the powers of these ancient giants, in such ways as I do not understand well. These heathens also believe in many gods, who are also themselves giants, and who also have power. But the giants of which Herger spoke were giant men, and not gods, or so it seemed to me.

That night we beached upon a rocky shore, made of stones the size of a man's fist, and there Buliwyf encamped with his men, and long into the night they drank and sang around the fire. Herger joined in the celebration and had no patience to explain to me the meaning of the songs, and so I do not know what they sang, but they were happy. On the morrow they would come to the home of Buliwyf, the land called Yatlam.

We left before the first light of dawn, and it was so cold my bones ached, and my body was sore from the rocky beach, and we set out upon the raging sea and the blasting wind. For all the morning we sailed, and during this period the excitement of the men increased further until they became like children or women. It was a wonder to me to see these huge strong warriors giggle and laugh like the Caliph's harem, and yet they saw nothing unmanly in this.

There was a point of land, a high rocky outcrop of gray stone above the gray sea, and beyond this point, Herger told me, would be the town of Yatlam. I strained to see this fabled home of Buliwyf as the Northmen's vessel came around the cliff. The warriors laughed and cheered more loudly, and I gathered there were many rude jokes and plans for sport with women when they landed.

And then there was the smell of smoke on the sea, and we saw smoke, and all the men fell silent. As we came around the point, I saw with my own eyes that the town there was in smoldering flames and billowing black smoke. There was no sign of life.

Buliwyf and his warriors landed and walked the town of Yatlam. There were dead bodies of men and women and children, some consumed by flames, some hacked by swords —a multitude of corpses. Buliwyf and the warriors did not speak and yet even here there was no grief, no crying and sadness. Never have I seen a race that accepts death as the Northmen do. I myself was sick many times at the sights, and they were never so.

At last I said to Herger, "Who has done this?" Herger pointed in to the land, to the forests and the hills set back from the gray ocean. There were mists over the forests. He pointed and did not speak. I said to him, "Is it the mists?" He said to me, "Do not ask more. You will know sooner than you wish."

Now this happened: Buliwyf entered one smoking ruined house and returned to our company bearing a sword. This sword was very large and heavy, and so heated by the fire that he carried it with a cloth wrapped around the handle. Verily I say it was the largest sword I have ever seen. It was as long as my own body and the blade was flat and broad as the palms of two men's hands set side by side. It was so large and heavy that even Buliwyf grunted at the carrying of it. I asked Herger what was the sword, and he said, "That is Runding," and then Buliwyf ordered all his party to the boat, and we set out to sea again. None of the warriors looked back at the burning town of Yatlam; I alone did this, and I saw the smoking ruin, and the mists in the hills beyond.

The encampment at Trelburg

For the space of two days we sailed along a flat coast among many islands that are called the land of Dans, coming finally to a region of marsh with a crisscross of narrow rivers that pour onto the sea. These rivers have no names themselves but are each one called "wyk," and the peoples of the narrow rivers are called "wykings," which means to the Northmen warriors who sail their ships up the rivers and attack settlements in such fashion.*

Now in this marshy region we stopped at a place they called Trelburg, which was a wonder to me. Here is no town, but rather a military camp, and its people are warriors, with few women or children among them. The defenses of this camp of Trelburg are constructed with great care and skill of workmanship in the Roman fashion.

Trelburg lies at the joining point of two wyks, which then run to the sea. The main part of the town is encircled by a round earthwork wall, as tall as five men standing one atop the other. Above this earthen ring there stands a wooden

---

* There is some dispute among modern scholars about the origin of the term "Viking," but most agree with Ibn Fadlan, that it derives from "vik," meaning a creek or narrow river.

fence for greater protection. Outside the earthen ring there is a ditch filled with water, the depth I do not know.

These earthworks are excellently made, of a symmetry and quality to rival anything we know. And there is this further: on the landward side of the town, a second semi-circle of high wall, and a second ditch beyond.

The town itself lies within the inner ring, which is broken by four gates, facing the four corners of the earth. Each gate is barred by strong oaken doors with heavy fittings of iron, and many guards. Many guards also walk the ramparts, keeping watch day and night.

Inside the town stand sixteen wooden dwellings, all the same: they are long houses, for so the Northmen call them, with walls that curve so that they resemble overturned boats with the ends cut flat front and back. In length they are thirty paces, and wider in the middle portion than either end. They are arranged thus: four long houses precisely set, so as to form a square. Four squares are arranged to make sixteen houses in all.*

Every long house has but one entrance, and no house has its entrance within sight of another. I inquired why this was so, and Herger said thus: "If the camp is attacked, the men must run to defense, and the doorways are such that the men can hasten without mingling and confusion, but on the contrary each man can proceed freely to the task of defense."

* The accuracy of Ibn Fadlan's reporting is confirmed here by direct archaeological evidence. In 1948 the military site of Trelleborg, in western Zealand in Denmark, was excavated. The site corresponds exactly to Ibn Fadlan's description of the size, nature, and structure of the settlement.

Thus it is within the square that one house has a north door, the next house an east door, the next house a south door, the next house a west door; so also each of the four squares.

Then also I saw that while the Northmen are gigantic, these doorways were so low that even I must bend in two to enter one of the houses. I inquired of Herger, who said: "If we are attacked, a single warrior may remain inside the house, and with his sword cut off the heads of all who enter. The door is low so that heads will be bent for cutting."

Verily, I saw that in all respects, the Trelburg town was constructed for warfare and for defense. No trading is conducted here at all, as I have said. Inside the long houses, there are three sections or rooms, each with a door. The center room is the largest, and it also has a pit for rubbish.

Now I saw that the Trelburg people were not as the Northmen along the Volga. These were clean people for their race. They washed in the river, and relieved their waste out of doors, and were in all ways much superior to what I had known. Yet they are not truly clean, except in comparison.

The society of Trelburg is mostly men, and the women are all slaves. There are no wives among the women, and all women are taken freely as the men desire. The people of Trelburg live on fish, and some little bread; they do no agriculture or farming, although the marshlands surrounding the town contain areas suitable for growing. I asked of Herger why there was no agriculture, and he said to me, "These are warriors. They do not till the soil."

Buliwyf and his company were graciously received by the chiefs of Trelburg, who are several, foremost among them one who is called Sagard. Sagard is a strong and fierce man, almost as huge as Buliwyf himself.

During the night banquet, Sagard inquired of Buliwyf his mission and the reasons for his travels, and Buliwyf reported of the supplication of Wulfgar. Herger translated all for me, although in truth I had spent sufficient time among these heathens to learn a word or two in their tongue. Here is the meaning of the conversation of Sagard and Buliwyf.

Sagard spoke thus: "It is sensible for Wulfgar to carry out the errand of a messenger, though he is the son of the King Rothgar, for the several sons of Rothgar have set upon one another."

Buliwyf said that he did not know of this, or words to that meaning. But I perceived that he was not greatly surprised. Yet it is true that Buliwyf was seldom surprised by any thing. Such was his role as leader of the warriors and hero to them.

Sagard spoke again: "Indeed, Rothgar had five sons, and three are dead at the hand of one of them, Wiglif, a cunning man,* whose conspirator in this affair is the herald of the old King. Only Wulfgar remains faithful, and he has departed."

Buliwyf said to Sagard that he was glad to know of this

---

* Literally, "a two-handed man." As will be clear later, the Northmen were ambidextrous in fighting, and to shift weapons from one hand to another was considered an admirable trick. Thus a two-handed man is cunning. A related meaning was once attached to the word "shifty," which now means deceitful and evasive, but formerly had a more positive sense of "resourceful, full of maneuvers."

news, and would hold it in his mind, and there the conversation ended. Never did Buliwyf or any of his warriors show surprise at the words of Sagard, and from this I took that it is ordinary for the sons of a king to dispose of one another to gain the throne.

Also it is true that from time to time a son may murder his father the king to gain the throne, and this is likewise counted nothing remarkable, for the Northmen see it the same as any drunken brawl among warriors. The Northmen have a proverb which is "Look to your back," and they believe that a man must always be prepared to defend himself, even a father against his own son.

Upon our departure, I inquired of Herger why there should be another fortification on the landward side of Trelburg, and yet no such additional fortification on the seaward side. These Northmen are seafaring men who attack from the sea, and yet Herger said, "It is the land that is dangerous."

I asked of him, "Why is the land dangerous?" And he replied, "Because of the mists."

Upon our departure from Trelburg, the warriors assembled there beat their staves upon their shields, raising a loud noise for our ship which set sail. This, I was told, was to draw the attention of Odin, one of the number of their gods, so that this Odin would look with favor upon the journey of Buliwyf and his twelve men.

Also, this I learned: that the number thirteen is significant to the Norsemen, because the moon grows and dies thirteen times in the passage of one year, by their reckoning. For this reason, all important accountings must include the number thirteen. Thus Herger said to me that the number of dwellings in Trelburg was thirteen and also three more, instead of sixteen, as I have expressed it.

Further, I learned that these Northmen have some notion that the year does not fit with exactitude into thirteen passages of the moon, and thus the number thirteen is not stable and fixed in their minds. The thirteenth passage is called magical and foreign, and Herger says, "Thus for the thirteenth man you were chosen as foreign."

Verily these Northmen are superstitious, with no recourse to sense or reason or law. They seemed to my eyes to be fierce children, and yet I was among them, and so held my tongue. Soon enough I was glad for my discretion, for these events followed:

We were sailing some time from Trelburg when I recalled that never previously had the inhabitants of a town made a departure ceremony with beating of shields to call up Odin. I spoke as much to Herger.

"It is true," he responded. "There is a special reason for the call to Odin, for we are now upon the sea of monsters."

This seemed to me proof of their superstition. I inquired if any of the warriors had ever seen such monsters. "Indeed, we have all seen them," Herger said. "Why else should we know of them?" By the tone of his voice, I could recognize that he thought me a fool for my disbelief.

Some further time passed, when there was a shout, and all the warriors of Buliwyf stood pointing to the sea, watching, shouting amongst themselves. I asked Herger what had happened. "We are among the monsters now," he said, pointing.

Now the ocean in this region is most turbulent. The wind blows with fierce force, turning the curls of the sea white with foam, spitting water into the face of a sailor, and playing tricks with his sight. I watched the sea for many minutes and had no view of this sea monster, and I had no reason to believe what they said.

Then one of their number shouted to Odin, a scream of prayer, repeating the name many times in supplication, and then I also saw with my own eyes the sea monster. It was in the shape of a giant snake that never raised its head above the surface, yet I saw its body curl and twist over, and it was very long, and wider than the Northmen's boat, and black in color. The sea monster spat water into the air, like a fountain, and then plunged down, raising a tail that was cleft in two, like the forked tongue of a snake. Yet it was enormous, each section of the tail being broader than the largest palm frond.

Now I saw another monster, and another, and another after that; there appeared to be four and perhaps six or seven. Each behaved as his fellows, curving through the water, spitting a fountain, and raising a giant tail split in two. At the sight, the Northmen shouted to Odin for aid, and not a few of their number fell to their knees on the deck trembling.

Verily I saw with my own eyes the sea monsters all about us in the ocean, and then, after some time had passed, they were gone and we did not see them again. The warriors of

Buliwyf resumed their sailing efforts, and no man spoke of the monsters, but I was much afraid long afterward, and Herger told me that my face was white as the face of a North person, and he laughed. "What does Allah say to this?" he asked of me, and to that I had no answer.*

In the evening, we beached and made a fire, and I inquired of Herger if the sea monsters ever attacked a ship on the sea, and if so, what was the manner of it, for I had seen the heads of none of these monsters.

Herger answered by calling Ethgow, one of the nobles and the lieutenant of Buliwyf. Ethgow was a solemn warrior who was not merry except when drunk. Herger said that he had been on a ship that was attacked. Ethgow said this to me: that the sea monsters are larger than anything on the surface of the land, and larger than any ship on the sea, and when they attack they ride under a ship and lift it in the air, and toss it aside like a bit of wood, and crush it with their forked tongue. Ethgow said that there had been thirty men on his ship, and only he and two others beside had survived, by the graciousness of the gods. Ethgow spoke in an ordinary manner of talking, which for him was very serious, and I believed him to be speaking the truth.

Also Ethgow told me that the Northmen know that the

---

* This account of what is obviously a sighting of whales is disputed by many scholars. It appears in the manuscript of Razi as it is here, but in Sjögren's translation it is much briefer, and in it the Northmen are shown as playing an elaborate joke upon the Arab. The Northmen knew about whales and distinguished them from sea monsters, according to Sjögren. Other scholars, including Hassan, doubt that Ibn Fadlan could be unaware of the existence of whales, as he appears to be here.

monsters attack ships because they desire to mate with the ship, mistaking it for one of their own. For this reason, the Northmen do not build their ships over-large.

Herger said to me that Ecthgow is a great warrior renowned in battle, and that he is to be believed in all things.

For the next two days, we sailed among the islands of the Dan country, and then on the third day we crossed a passage of open water. Here I was afraid to see more of the sea monsters, but we did not, and eventually arrived at the territory called Venden. These lands of Venden are mountainous and forbidding, and the men of Buliwyf in his boat approached with some trepidation and the killing of a hen, which was thrown into the ocean thus: the head was thrown from the bow of the ship, and the body of the hen was thrown from the stern, near the helmsman.

We did not beach directly on this new land of Venden, but sailed along the coast, coming at last to the kingdom of Rothgar. I first saw it thus. High upon a cliff, commanding a view of the raging gray sea, was a huge great hall of wood, strong and imposing. I said to Herger it was a magnificent sight, but Herger and all his company, led by Buliwyf, were groaning and shaking their heads. I inquired of Herger why this was so. He said, "Rothgar is called Rothgar the Vain, and his great hall is the mark of a vain man."

I said, "Why do you speak thus? Because of its size and splendor?" For verily, as we came closer, I saw that the hall was richly ornamented with carvings and silver chasing, which sparkled from a distance.

"No," said Herger. "I say that Rothgar is vain because of

the way he has placed his settlement. He dares the gods to strike him down, and he pretends he is more than a man, and so he is punished."

Never have I seen a more impregnable great hall, and I said to Herger, "This hall cannot be attacked; how can Rothgar be struck down?"

Herger laughed at me, and said thus: "You Arabs are stupid beyond counting, and know nothing of the ways of the world. Rothgar deserves the misfortune that has come to him, and it is only we who shall save him, and perhaps not even so."

These words puzzled me further. I looked at Ecthgow, the lieutenant of Buliwyf, and saw that he stood in the boat and made a brave face, and yet his knees trembled, and it was not the stiffness of the wind that made them tremble so. He was afraid; they were all afraid; and I did not know why.

The kingdom of Rothgar in the land of Venden

The ship was beached at the time of the afternoon prayer, and I begged the forgiveness of Allah for not making supplication. Yet I had not been able to do so in the presence of the Northmen, who thought my prayers to be a curse upon them, and threatened to kill me if I prayed in their sight.

Each warrior in the boat dressed in the garments of battle, which were thus: first, boots and leggings of rough wool, and over this a coat of heavy fur, which reached to the knees. Over this they placed coats of mail, which all had save me. Then each man took his sword and clasped it to his belt; each man took up his white shield of hide, and his spear; each man placed a helmet of metal or leather upon his head;* in this all the men were the same except for Buliwyf, who alone carried his sword in his hand, so large was it.

The warriors looked up to the great hall of Rothgar, and marveled at its gleaming roof and skilled workmanship, and

---

* Popular representations of the Scandinavians always show them wearing helmets with horns. This is an anachronism; at the time of Ibn Fadlan's visit, such helmets had not been worn for more than a thousand years, since the Early Bronze Age.

74

agreed that there was none like it in the world, with its lofty gables and rich carving. Yet there was no respect in their speech.

At length we decamped from the ship, and traveled a road paved in stone up to the great hall. The clanking of swords and the clatter of mail raised a goodly noise. After we had gone some short distance, we saw by the roadway the severed head of an ox, set upon a stick. This animal was freshly killed.

All the Northmen sighed and made sad faces at this portent, though it had no meaning to me. I was by now adjusted to their custom of killing some beast at the slightest nervousness or provocation. Yet this oxhead had especial significance.

Buliwyf looked away, across the fields of the lands of Rothgar, and saw there an isolated farming house, of the sort that is common in Rothgar lands. The walls of this house were of wood, and sealed with a paste of mud and straw, which must be replenished after the frequent rains. The roof is thatched material and wood also. Inside the houses there is only an earthen floor and a hearth, and the dung of animals, for the farm people sleep with their animals indoors for the warmth afforded by their bodies, and then they burn the dung for fires.

Buliwyf gave an order that we should go to this farmhouse, and so we set out across the fields, which were verdant but soggy with dampness underfoot. Once or twice the company halted to examine the ground before continuing on, but they never saw anything that mattered to them. I myself saw nothing.

Yet again Buliwyf halted his company, and pointed to the

dark earth. Verily, I saw with my own eyes the bare imprint of a foot—indeed, of many feet. They were flat and uglier than anything known to creation. At each toe, there was the sharp digging mark of a horned nail or claw; thus the shape appeared human, but yet not human. This I saw with my own eyes, and could scarcely believe the witness of my sight.

Buliwyf and his warriors shook their heads at the sight, and I heard them repeat one word over and over: "wendol" or "wendlon," or some such. The meaning of the name was not known to me, and I sensed that Herger should not be asked at this moment, for he was as apprehensive as all the rest. We pressed on to the farmhouse, now and again seeing more of these horned footprints in the earth. Buliwyf and his warriors walked slowly, but it was not caution; no man drew his weapon; rather it was some dread that I did not comprehend and yet felt with them.

At length we came to the farming dwelling and entered it. In the farmhouse I saw, with my own eyes, this sight: there was a man, of young age and graceful proportion, whose body had been torn limb from limb. The torso was here, an arm there, a leg there. Blood lay in thick pools upon the floor, and on the walls, on the roof, on every surface in such profusion that the house seemed to have been painted in red blood. Also there was a woman, in like fashion rended limb from limb. Also a male child, an infant of two years or less, whose head was wrenched from the shoulders, leaving the body a bleeding stump.

All this I saw with my own eyes, and it was the most fearsome sight I ever witnessed. I purged myself and was faint for an hour, purging myself yet again.

Eaters of the Dead

Never will I comprehend the manner of the Northmen, for even as I was sick, so they became calm and dispassionate at the aspect of this horror; they viewed all they saw in quiet fashion; they discussed the claw marks upon the limbs, and the manner of tearing of flesh. Much attention was given to the fact that all the heads were missing; also, they remarked the most devilish aspect of all, which even now I recall with trepidation.

The body of the male child had been chewed by some fiendish teeth, upon the soft flesh of the back of the thigh. So also had been chewed the area of the shoulder. This very horror I saw with my own eyes.

The warriors of Buliwyf were grim-countenanced and glowering as they departed the farmhouse. They continued to pay much heed to the soft earth about the house, noting that there were no hoofmarks of horses; this was a matter of significance to them. I did not understand why. Nor was I much attentive, still feeling faint of heart and sick of body.

As we crossed the fields, Ecthgow made a discovery which was of this nature: it was a small bit of stone, smaller than a child's fist, and it was polished and carved in crude fashion. All the warriors crowded around to examine it, I among them.

I saw it to be the torso of a pregnant female. There was no head, no arms, and no legs; only the torso with a greatly swollen belly and, above that, two pendulous swollen breasts.* I accounted this creation exceedingly crude and ugly, but nothing more. Yet the Northmen were suddenly overcome

* The described figurine corresponds closely to several carvings discovered by archaeologists in France and Austria.

and pale and tremulous; their hands shook to touch it, and
finally Buliwyf flung it to the ground and shattered it with
the handle of his sword, until it lay in splintered stone
fragments. And then were several of the warriors sick, and
purged themselves upon the ground. And the general horror
was very great, to my mystification.

Now they set off for the great hall of King Rothgar. No
man spoke during our travel, which was the better part of an
hour; every one of the Northmen seemed to be wrapped in
bitter and consuming thought, and yet they showed no fear
anymore.

At length, a herald upon a horse met us and barred our
path. He noted the arms we carried and the bearing of the
company and of Buliwyf, and shouted a warning.

Herger said to me, "He craves to know our names, and
curtly, too."

Buliwyf made some answer to the herald, and from his
tone I knew that Buliwyf was in no mood for courtly plea-
santries. Herger said to me: "Buliwyf tells him we are sub-
jects of King Higlac, of the kingdom of Yatlam, and we are
on an errand to the King Rothgar, and would speak to him."
And Herger added, "Buliwyf says that Rothgar is a most
worthy king," but the tone of Herger conveyed the opposite
sense of the matter.

This herald bade us continue to the great hall and wait
outside while he told the King of our arrival. This we did,
although Buliwyf and his party were not pleased at such
treatment; there was grumbling and muttering, for it is the
Northman's way to be hospitable and this did not seem

gracious, to be kept outside. Yet they waited, and also removed their weapons, their swords and spears, but not their
armor, and they left the weapons outside the doors to the
hall.

Now the hall was surrounded on all sides by several dwellings in the fashion of the North people. These were long
with curved sides, as at Trelburg; but they differed in the
arrangement, for there were no squares here. Nor were there
fortifications or earthworks to be seen. Rather, from the great
hall and the long houses about it, the ground sloped to a
long flat green plain, here and there a farmhouse, and then,
beyond, the hills and the edge of a forest.

I inquired of Herger whose long houses were these, and he
said to me, "Some belong to the King, and others are for his
royal family, and others for his nobles, and also for the servants and lower members of his court." He said also that it
was a difficult place, though I did not comprehend his meaning in this.

Then we were allowed entry into the great hall of King
Rothgar, which verily I say is to be counted one of the
marvels of all the world, and all the more for its presence in
the crude North country. This hall is called, among the
Rothgar peoples, by the name of Hurot, for the Northmen
give the names of people to the things of their life, to the
buildings and boats and especially to the weapons. Now I
say: this Hurot, the great hall of Rothgar, was as large as the
Caliph's main palace, and richly inlaid with silver and even
some gold, which is most rare in the North. On all sides
were designs and ornaments of the greatest splendor and

richness of artistry. It was truly a monument to the power and majesty of King Rothgar.

This King Rothgar sat at the distant end of Hurot Hall, a space so vast that he was so far we could hardly discern him. Standing behind his right shoulder was the same herald who had halted us. The herald made a speech, which Herger told me was thus: "Here, O King, is a band of warriors from the kingdom of Yatlam. They are newly arrived from the sea, and their leader is a man of the name Buliwyf. They beg leave to tell you of their errand, O King. Do not forbid them entry; they have the manner of earls, and from his bearing their chieftain is a mighty warrior. Greet them as earls, O King Rothgar."

Thus we were bid approach the King Rothgar.

King Rothgar appeared a man near death. He was not young, his hair was white, his skin was very pale, and his face was grooved with sorrow and fear. He regarded us with suspicion, wrinkling his eyes, or perhaps he was near blind, I do not know. Finally he broke into a speech, which Herger says was thus: "I know of this man, for I have sent for him on a hero's mission. He is Buliwyf, and I knew him as a child, when I traveled across the waters to the kingdom of Yatlam. He is the son of Higlac, who was my gracious host, and now this son comes to me in my time of need and sorrow."

Rothgar then called for the warriors to be summoned to the great hall, and gifts brought, and celebrations made.

Buliwyf then spoke, a long speech that Herger did not translate for me, since to speak when Buliwyf spoke would be a disrespect. However, the meaning was this: that Buliwyf had heard of the troubles of Rothgar, that he was sorry for these troubles, and that his own father's kingdom had been destroyed by these same troubles, and that he had come to save the kingdom of Rothgar from the evils that had beset them.

Still, I did not know what the Northmen called these evils, or how they thought of them, though I had viewed the handiwork of the beasts that tore men to pieces.

King Rothgar spoke again, in some haste. I took from the manner of his speaking that he wished to say some words before all his warriors and earls arrived. He said thus (from Herger): "O Buliwyf, I knew your father when I was myself a young man, new to my throne. Now I am old and heartsick. My head bows. My eyes weep with shame to acknowledge my weakness. As you see, my throne is almost a barren spot. My lands are becoming a wild place. What the fiends have wrought to my kingdom I cannot say. Often at night, my warriors, brave with drink, swear to topple the fiends. And then when the bleak light of dawn creeps over the misty fields, we see bloody bodies everywhere. Thus is the sorrow of my life, and I shall speak no more of it."

Now a bench was brought out and a meal set before us, and I inquired of Herger what was the meaning of the "fiends" of which the King spoke. Herger was angry, and said I was never to ask again.

That evening there was a great celebration, and King Rothgar and his Queen Weilew, in a garment dripping gemstones and gold, presided over the nobles and warriors and

Eaters of the Dead

earls of the kingdom of Rothgar. These nobles were a paltry
lot; they were old men and drank overmuch and many were
crippled or wounded. In the eyes of all of them was the
hollow stare of fear, and there was hollowness in their merriment, too.

Also there was the son named Wiglif, of whom I have
earlier spoken, the son of Rothgar who murdered three of
his brothers. This man was young and slender with a blond
beard and with eyes that never settled on anything, but
moved about here and there constantly; also he never met
the gaze of another. Herger saw him and said, "He is a fox."
By this he meant that he was a slippery and changeable person of false demeanor, for the North people believe the fox is
an animal that can assume any form it pleases.

Now, in the middle portion of the festivities, Rothgar sent
his herald to the doors of Hurot Hall, and this herald reported that the mist would not descend that night. There was
much happiness and celebration over this announcement that
the night was clear; all were pleased save Wiglif.

At a particular time, the son Wiglif rose to his feet and
said, "I drink honor to our guests, and especially Buliwyf, a
brave and true warrior who has come to aid us in our plight
—although it may prove too great an obstacle for him to overcome." Herger whispered these words to me, and I caught
that it was praise and insult in one breath.

All eyes turned to Buliwyf for his response. Buliwyf stood,
and looked to Wiglif, and then said, "I have no fear of anything, even the callow fiend that creeps at night to murder
men in their sleep." This I took to refer to the "wendol," but
Wiglif turned pale and gripped the chair in which he sat.

82

"Do you speak of me?" Wiglif said, in a trembling tongue.

Buliwyf made this response: "No, but I do not fear you any more than the monsters of the mist."

The young man Wiglif persisted, although Rothgar the King called for him to be seated. Wiglif said to all the assembled nobles: "This Buliwyf, arrived from foreign shores, has by appearance great pride and great strength. Yet have I arranged to test his mettle, for pride may cover any man's eyes."

Now I saw this thing happen: a strong warrior, seated at a table near the door, behind Buliwyf, rose with speed, plucked up a spear, and charged at the back of Buliwyf. All this happened in less time than it takes a man to suck in his breath.* Yet also Buliwyf turned, plucked up a spear, and with this he caught the warrior full into the chest, and lifted him by the shaft of the spear high over his head and flung him against a wall. Thus was this warrior skewered on the spear, his feet dangling above the floor, kicking; the shaft of the spear was buried into the wall of the hall of Hurot. The warrior died without a sound.

Now there came much commotion, and Buliwyf turned to face Wiglif, and said, "So shall I dispatch any menace," and then with great immediacy Herger spoke, in an overloud voice, and made many gestures toward my person. I was much confused by these events, and in truth my eyes were stuck upon this dead warrior pinned to the wall.

Then Herger turned to me, and said in Latin, "You shall sing a song for the court of King Rothgar. All desire it."

* *Ducere spiritu:* literally, "to inhale."

I asked of him, "What shall I sing? I know no song." He made this reply: "You will sing something that entertains the heart." And he added, "Do not speak of your one God. No one cares for such nonsense."

In truth, I did not know what to sing, for I am no minstrel. A time passed while all stared toward me, and there was silence in the hall. Then Herger said to me, "Sing a song of kings and valor in battle."

I said that I knew no such songs, but that I could tell them a fable, which in my country was accounted funny and entertaining. To this he said that I had made a wise choice. Then I told them—King Rothgar, his Queen Weilew, his son Wiglif, and all the assembled earls and warriors—the story of Abu Kassim's slippers, which all know. I spoke lightly, and smiled all the while, and in the first instance the Northmen were pleased, and laughed and slapped their bellies.

But now this strange event occurred. As I continued in my telling, the Northmen ceased to laugh, and turned gloomy by degrees, ever more so, and when I had finished the tale, there was no laughter, but dire silence.

Herger said to me, "You could not know, but that is no tale for laughter, and now I must make amends," and thereupon he said some speech that I took to be a joke at my own expense, and there was general laughter, and at length the celebration recommenced.

> The story of Abu Kassim's slippers is ancient in Arabic culture, and was well known to Ibn Fadlan and his fellow Bagdad citizens.

The story exists in many versions, and can be told briefly or elaborately, depending upon the enthusiasm of the teller. Briefly, Abu Kassim is a rich merchant and a miser who wishes to hide the fact of his wealth, in order to strike better bargains in his trade. To give the appearance of poverty, he wears a pair of particularly tawdry, miserable slippers, hoping that people will be fooled, but nobody is. Instead, the people around him think he is silly and preposterous.

One day, Abu Kassim strikes a particularly favorable bargain in glassware, and decides to celebrate, not in the accepted manner of treating his friends to a feast, but by treating himself to the small selfish luxury of a visit to the public baths. He leaves his clothes and shoes in the anteroom, and a friend berates him for his worn and inappropriate shoes. Abu Kassim replies that they are still serviceable, and he enters the bath with his friend. Later, a powerful judge also comes to the baths, and disrobes, leaving behind an elegant pair of slippers. Meanwhile, Abu Kassim departs from the bath and cannot find his old slippers; in their place he finds a new and beautiful pair of shoes, and, presuming these to be a present from his friend, he puts them on and leaves.

When the judge leaves, his own slippers are missing, and all he can find are a miserable, tawdry pair of slippers, which everyone knows belong to the miser Abu Kassim. The judge is angry; servants are dispatched to retrieve the missing slippers; and they are soon found upon the very feet of the thief, who is hauled into court before the magistrate and severely fined.

Abu Kassim curses his bad luck, and once home flings the unlucky slippers out of his window, where they fall into the muddy Tigris River. Some days later, a group of fishermen haul in their catch, and find along with some fish the slippers of Abu Kassim; the hobnails of these slippers have

85

torn their nets. Enraged, they throw the soggy slippers through an open window. The window happens to be that of Abu Kassim; the slippers fall upon the newly purchased glassware and smash it all.

Abu Kassim is heartbroken, and grieves as only a stingy miser can. He vows the wretched slippers shall do him no further harm and, to be certain, goes to his garden with a shovel and buries them. As it happens, his next-door neighbor sees Abu Kassim digging, a menial task fit only for a servant. The neighbor assumes that if the master of the house is doing this chore himself, it must be in order to bury treasure. Thus the neighbor goes to the Caliph and informs on Abu Kassim, for according to the laws of the land, any treasure found in the ground is the property of the Caliph.

Abu Kassim is called before the Caliph, and when he reports that he buried only a pair of old slippers, the court laughs uproariously at the obviousness of the merchant's attempt to conceal his true, and illegal, purpose. The Caliph is angry to be thought such a fool as to be given this silly lie, and increases the magnitude of his fine accordingly. Abu Kassim is thunderstruck when sentence is passed, and yet he is obliged to pay.

Abu Kassim is now determined to be rid of his slippers once and for all. To be certain of no further trouble, he makes a pilgrimage far from town and drops the slippers into a distant pond, watching them sink to the bottom with satisfaction. But the pond feeds the city's water supply, and eventually the slippers clog the pipes; guards dispatched to release the stricture find the slippers and recognize them, for everyone knows the slippers of this notorious miser. Abu Kassim is again brought before the Caliph, on a charge of befouling the water of the town, and his fine is much greater than before. The slippers are returned to him.

Now Abu Kassim determines to burn the slippers, but they are still wet, so he sets them on the balcony to dry. A dog sees them and plays with them; one of the slippers falls from his jaws and drops to the street far below, where it strikes a woman passing by. The woman is pregnant, and the force of the blow causes a miscarriage. Her husband runs to the court to seek damages, which are awarded plentifully, and Abu Kassim, now a broken and impoverished man, is obliged to pay.

The slyly literal Arabic moral states that this story illustrates what evils can befall a man who does not change his slippers often enough. But undoubtedly the undercurrent to the tale, the idea of a man who cannot shake off some burden, was what disturbed the Northmen.

Now the night passed with further celebrations, and all the warriors of Buliwyf disported in a carefree fashion. I saw the son Wiglif glaring at Buliwyf before leaving the hall, but Buliwyf paid no attention, preferring the ministrations of slave girls and freeborn women. After a time I slept.

In the morning, I awoke to the sounds of hammering and, venturing from the great hall of Hurot, I found all the peoples of the kingdom of Rothgar at work on defenses. These were being laid out in preliminary fashion: horses drew up quantities of fence posts, which warriors sharpened to points; Buliwyf himself directed the placement of defense works, by marking scratches in the ground with the tip of his sword. For this he did not use his great sword Runding, but rather some other sword; I do not know if there was a reason for this.

Upon the middle portion of the day, the woman who was called the angel of death* came and cast bones on the ground, and made incantations over them, and announced that the mist would come that night. Upon hearing this, Buliwyf called for all work to cease, and a great banquet to be prepared. In this matter, all the people concurred, and ceased their efforts. I inquired of Herger why there should be a banquet, but he replied to me that I had too many questions. It is also true that I had timed my inquiry badly, for he was posturing before a blond slave girl who smiled warmly in his direction.

Now, in the later part of the day, Buliwyf called together all his warriors and said to them, "Prepare for battle," and they agreed, and wished luck one to another, while all about us the banquet was being made ready.

The night banquet was much as the previous one, although there were fewer of Rothgar's nobles and earls. Indeed, I learned that many nobles would not attend at all, for fear of what would happen in the Hurot Hall that night, for it seemed that this place was the center of the fiend's interest in the area; that he coveted Hurot Hall, or some similar thing—I could not be sure of the meaning.

This banquet was not enjoyable to me, for reason of my apprehension of coming events. However, this event occurred: one of the elderly nobles spoke some Latin, and also

---

* This is not the same "angel of death" who was with the Northmen on the banks of the Volga. Apparently each tribe had an old woman who performed shamanistic functions and was referred to as "the angel of death." It is thus a generic term.

some of the Iberian dialects, for he had traveled to the region of the caliphate of Cordova as a younger man, and I engaged him in conversation. In this circumstance, I feigned knowledge that I did not have, as you shall see.

He spoke to me thus: "So you are the foreigner who shall be the number thirteen?" And I said that I was such. "You must be exceedingly brave," the old man said, "and for your bravery I salute you." To this I made some trifling polite response, of the sense that I was a coward compared to the others of Buliwyf's company; which indeed was more than true.

"No matter," said the old man, who was deep in his cups, having drunk the liquor of the region—a vile substance they call mead, yet it is potent—"you are still a brave man to face the wendol."

Now I sensed that I might finally learn some matters of substance. I repeated to this old man a saying of the Northmen, which Herger had once said to me. I said, "Animals die, friends die, and I shall die, but one thing never dics, and that is the reputation we leave behind at our death."

The old man cackled toothlessly at this; he was pleased I knew a Northman proverb. He said, "That is so, but the wendol have a reputation, too." And I replied, with the utmost indifference: "Truly? I am not aware of it."

At this the old man said that I was a foreigner, and he would consent to enlighten me, and he told me this: the name of "wendol," or "windon," is a very ancient name, as old as any of the peoples of the North country, and it means "the black mist." To the Northmen, this means a mist that brings, under cover of night, black fiends who murder and kill and eat the flesh of human beings.* The fiends are hairy and loathsome to touch and smell; they are fierce and cunning; they speak no language of any man and yet converse among themselves; they come with the night fog, and disappear by day—to where, no man durst follow.

The old man said to me thus: "You can know the regions where dwell the fiends of the black mist by many ways. From time to time, warriors on horse may hunt a stag with dogs, chasing the stag over hill and dale for many miles of forest and open land. And then the stag comes to some

* The Scandinavians were apparently more impressed by the stealth and viciousness of the creatures than the fact of their cannibalism. Jensen suggests that cannibalism might be abhorrent to the Norsemen because it made entry into Valhalla more difficult; there is no evidence for this view.

However, for Ibn Fadlan, with his extensive erudition, the notion of cannibalism may have implied some difficulties in the afterlife. The Eater of the Dead is a well-known creature of Egyptian mythology, a fearsome beast with the head of a crocodile, the trunk of a lion, and the back of a hippopotamus. This Eater of the Dead devours the wicked after their Judgment.

It is worth remembering that for most of man's history, ritual cannibalism, in one form or another, for one reason or another, was neither rare nor remarkable. Peking man and Neanderthal man were both apparently cannibals; so were, at various times, the Scythians, the Chinese, the Irish, the Peruvians, the Mayoruna, the Jagas, the Egyptians, the Australian aborigines, the Maoris, the Greeks, the Hurons, the Iroquois, the Pawnees, and the Ashanti.

During the time Ibn Fadlan was in Scandinavia, other Arab traders were in China, where they recorded that human flesh—referred to as "two-legged mutton"—was openly and legally sold in markets.

Martinson suggests that the Northmen found the wendol cannibalism repellent because they believed that the flesh of warriors was fed to women, particularly the mother of the wendol. There is no evidence for this view, either, but it would certainly make a Norse warrior's death more shameful.

marshy tarn or brackish swamp, and here it will halt, preferring to be torn to bits by the hounds rather than enter
that loathsome region. Thus we know of the areas where
the wendol live, and we know that even the animals will
not enter thence."

I expressed over-great wonderment at this tale, in order to
draw further words from the old man. Herger saw me then,
and gave me a menacing look, but I paid him no heed.

The old man continued thus: "In olden days, the black
mist was feared by all the Northmen of every region. Since
my father and his father and his father before, no Northman
has seen the black mist, and some of the young warriors
counted us old fools to remember the ancient tales of their
horror and depredations. Yet the chiefs of the Northmen in
all the kingdoms, even in Norway, have always been prepared for the return of the black mist. All of our towns and
our fortresses are protected and defended from the land.
Since the time of the father of my father's father, our peoples
have thus acted, and never have we seen the black mist. Now
it has returned."

I inquired why the black mist had returned, and he lowered his voice to speak this reply: "The black mist has come
from the vanity and weakness of Rothgar, who has offended
the gods with his foolish splendor and tempted the fiends
with the siting of his great hall, which has no protection
from the land. Rothgar is old and he knows he will not be
remembered for battles fought and won, and so he built
this splendid hall, which is the talk of all the world, and
pleases his vanity. Rothgar acts as a god, yet he is a man,

and the gods have sent the black mist to strike him down and show him humility."

I said to this old man that perhaps Rothgar was resented in the kingdom. He replied thus: "No man is so good as to be free from all evil, nor so bad as to be worth nothing. Rothgar is a just king and his people prospered all of his life. The wisdom and richness of his rule are here, in Hurot Hall, and they are splendid. His only fault is this, that he forgot defense, for we have a saying among us: 'A man should never move a step from his weapons.' Rothgar has no weapons; he is toothless and weak; and the black mist seeps freely over the land."

I desired to know more, but the old man was tired, and turned away from me, and soon was asleep. Verily, the food and drink of Rothgar's hospitality were much, and many of the number of earls and nobles were drowsy.

Of the table of Rothgar I shall say this: that every man had a tablecloth and plate, and spoon and knife; that the meal was boiled pork and goat, and some fish, too, for the Northmen much prefer boiled meat to roasted. Then there were cabbages and onions in abundance, and apples and hazelnuts. A sweetish fleshy meat was given me that I had not tasted before; this, I was told, was elk, or rain-deer.

The dreadful foul drink called mead is made from honey, then fermented. It is the sourest, blackest, vilest stuff ever invented by any man, and yet it is potent beyond all knowing; a few drinks, and the world spins. But I did not drink, praise Allah.

Now I noticed that Buliwyf and all his company did not

drink that night, or only sparingly, and Rothgar took this as no insult, but rather acknowledged it as the natural course of things. There was no wind that night; the candles and flames of Hurot Hall did not flicker, and yet it was damp, and chill. I saw with my own eyes that out of doors the mist was rolling in from the hills, blocking the silvered light of the moon, cloaking all in blackness.

As the night continued, King Rothgar and his Queen departed for sleep, and the massive doors of Hurot Hall were locked and barred, and the nobles and earls remaining there fell into a drunken stupor and snored loudly.

Then Buliwyf and his men, still wearing their armor, went about the room, dousing the candles and seeing to the fires, that they should burn low and weak. I asked Herger the meaning of this, and he told me to pray for my life, and to feign sleep. I was given a weapon, a short sword, but it was little comfort to me; I am not a warrior and know it full well.

Verily, all the men feigned sleep, Buliwyf and his men joined the slumbering bodies of the King Rothgar's earls, who were truly snoring. How long we waited I do not know, for I think I slept awhile myself. Then all at once I was awake, in a manner of unnatural sharp alertness; I was not drowsy but instantly tense and alert, still lying on a bearskin cloth on the floor of the great hall. It was dark night; the candles in the hall burned low, and a faint breeze whispered through the hall and fluttered the yellow flames.

And then I heard a low grunting sound, like the rooting of a pig, carried to me by the breeze, and I smelled a rank odor like the rot of a carcass after a month, and I feared greatly. This rooting sound, for I can call it none else, this grumbling, grunting, snorting sound, grew louder and more excited. It came from outdoors, at one side of the hall. Then I heard it from another side, and then another, and another. Verily the hall was surrounded.

I sat up on one elbow, my heart pounding, and I looked about the hall. No man among the sleeping warriors moved, and yet there was Herger, lying with his eyes wide open. And there, too, Buliwyf, breathing in a snore, with his eyes also wide open. From this I gathered that all the warriors of Buliwyf were waiting to do battle with the wendol, whose sounds now filled the air.

By Allah, there is no fear greater than that of a man when he does not know the cause. How long I lay upon the bear-skin, hearing the grunting of the wendol and smelling their foul odors! How long I waited for I knew not what, the start of some battle more fearsome in the prospect than it could be in the fighting! I remembered this: that the North-men have a saying of praise that they carve upon the tomb-stones of noble warriors, which is this: "He did not flee battle." None of the company of Buliwyf fled that night, though the sounds and the stink were all around them, now louder, now fainter, now from one direction, now another. And yet they waited.

Then came the most fearsome moment. All sounds ceased. There was utter silence, except for the snoring of the men and the low crackle of the fire. Still none of the warriors of Buliwyf stirred.

And then there was a mighty crash upon the solid doors of the hall of Hurot, and these doors burst open, and a rush of reeking air gutted all the lights, and the black mist entered the room. I did not count their number: verily it seemed thousands of black grunting shapes, and yet it might have been no more than five or six, huge black shapes hardly in the manner of men, and yet also manlike. The air stank of blood and death; I was cold beyond reason, and shivered. Yet still no warrior moved.

Then, with a curdling scream to wake the dead, Buliwyf leapt up, and in his arms he swung the giant sword Runding, which sang like a sizzling flame as it cut the air. And his warriors leapt up with him, and all joined the battle. The shouts of the men mingled with the pig-grunts and the odors of the black mist, and there was terror and confusion and great wracking and rending of the Hurot Hall.

I myself had no stomach for battle, and yet I was set upon by one of these mist monsters, who came close to me, and I saw gleaming red eyes—verily I saw eyes that shone like fire, and I smelled the reek, and I was lifted bodily and flung across the room as a child flings a pebble. I struck the wall and fell to the ground, and was greatly dazed for the next period, so all around me was more confused than true.

I remember, most distinctly, the touch of these monsters upon me, especially the furry aspect of the bodies, for these mist monsters have hair as long as a hairy dog, and as thick, on all parts of their bodies. And I remember the fetid smell of the breath of the monster who flung me.

The battle raged for how long I cannot know, but it concluded most suddenly of a moment. And then the black mist was gone, slunk away, grunting and panting and stinking, leaving behind destruction and death that we could not know until we had lighted fresh tapers.

Here is how the battle waged. Of the company of Buliwyf, three were dead, Roneth and Halga, both earls, and Edgtho, a warrior. The first had his chest torn open. The second had his spine broken. The third had his head torn off in the manner I had already witnessed. All these warriors were dead.

Wounded were two others, Haltaf and Rethel. Haltaf had lost an ear, and Rethel two fingers of his right hand. Both men were not mortally injured, and made no complaint, for it is the Northman way to bear the wounds of battle cheerfully, and to praise above all the retaining of life.

As for Buliwyf and Herger and all the others, they were soaked in blood as if they had bathed in it. Now I shall say what many will not believe, and yet it was so: our company had killed not one of the mist monsters. Each had slunk away, some perhaps mortally wounded, and yet they had escaped.

Herger said thus: "I saw two of their number carrying a third, who was dead." Perhaps this was so, for all generally agreed upon it. I learned that the mist monsters never leave one of their kind to the society of men, but rather will risk great dangers to retrieve him from human purview. So also will they go to extreme lengths to keep a victim's head, and we could not find the head of Edgtho in any place; the monsters had carried it off with them.

Then Buliwyf spoke, and Herger told me his words thus: "Look, I have retained a trophy of the night's bloody deeds. See, here is an arm of one of the fiends."

And, true to his word, Buliwyf held the arm of one of the mist monsters, cut off at the shoulder by the great sword Runding. All the warriors crowded around to examine it. I perceived it thusly: it appeared to be small, with a hand of abnormally large size. But the forearm and upper arm were not large to match it, although the muscles were powerful. There was long black matted hair on all parts of the arm except the palm of the hand. Finally it is to say that the arm stank as the whole beast stank, with the fetid smell of the black mist.

Now all the warriors cheered Buliwyf, and his sword Runding. The fiend's arm was hung from the rafters of the great hall of Hurot, and marveled at by all the people of the kingdom of Rothgar. Thus ended the first battle with the wendol.

The events that followed the first battle

Verily, the people of the North country never act as human beings of reason and sense. After the attack of the mist monsters, and their beating back by Buliwyf and his company, with me amongst them, the men of the kingdom of Rothgar did nothing.

There was no celebration, no feasting, no jubilation or display of happiness. From far and wide, the people of the kingdom came to view the dangling arm of the fiend, which hung in the great hall, and this they greeted with much amazement and astonishment. But Rothgar himself, the half-blind old man, expressed no pleasure, and presented Buliwyf and his company with no gifts, planned no feasts, gave him no slaves, no silver, no precious garments, or any other sign of honor.

Contrary to any expression of pleasure, King Rothgar made a long face and was solemn, and seemed more fearful than he had been before. I myself, though I did not speak it aloud, suspected that Rothgar preferred his earlier condition, before the black mist was beaten.

Nor was Buliwyf different in manner. He called for no

ceremonies, no feasting, no drinking or eating of food. The nobles who had died valiantly in the battle of the night were quickly placed in pits with a wooden roof over the top, and left there for the assigned ten days. There was haste in this matter.

Yet it was only in the laying out of the dead warriors that Buliwyf and his comrades showed happiness, or allowed themselves any smiles. After further time among the Northmen, I learned that they smile upon any death in battle, for this is pleasure taken on behalf of the dead person, and not the living. They are pleased when any man dies a warrior's death. Also the opposite is held true by them; they show distress when a man dies in his sleep, or in a bed. They say of such a man, "He died as a cow in the straw." This is no insult, but it is a reason for mourning the death.

The Northmen believe that how a man dies determines his condition in the afterlife, and they value the death of a warrior in battle above all. A "straw death" is shameful.

Any man who dies in his sleep is said by them to be strangled by the maran, or mare of the night. This creature is a woman, which makes such a death shameful, for to die at the hands of a woman is degrading above all things.

Also they say to die without your weapons is degrading, and a Northman warrior will always sleep with his weapons, so that if the maran comes at night, he will have his weapons at hand. Seldom does a warrior die of some illness, or of the enfeeblement of age. I heard of one king, of the name Ane, who lived to such an age that he became as an infant, toothless and existing upon the food of an infant, and he spent all his days in his bed drinking milk from a horn. But this was told to me as most uncommon in the North country. With my own eyes I saw few men grown very old, by which I mean grown old to the time when the beard is not only white but falling out from the chin and face.

Several of their women live to great age, especially such as the old crone they call the angel of death; these old women are counted as having magical powers in healing of wounds, casting of spells, banishing evil influences, and foretelling the future of events.

The women of the North people do not fight among themselves, and often did I see them intercede in a growing brawl or duel of two men, to quench the rising anger. This they will do especially if the warriors are thickened and slow with drink. This is often the circumstance.

Now, the Northmen, who drink much liquor, and at all hours of the day and night, drank nothing on the day after the battle. Seldom did the people of Rothgar offer them a cup, and when it happened, the cup was refused. This I found most puzzling, and spoke of it finally to Herger.

Herger shook his shoulders in the Northmen's gesture of unconcern, or indifference. "Everyone is afraid," he said.

I inquired why there should still be a reason to fear. He spoke thus: "It is because they know that the black mist will return."

Now I admit that I was puffed with the arrogance of a fighting man, though in truth I knew I did not deserve such a posture. Even so, I felt exhilaration at my survival, and the people of Rothgar treated me as one of a company of mighty warriors. I said boldly, "Who cares for that? If they come again, we shall beat them a second time."

Indeed, I was vain as a young cock, and I am abashed now to think upon my strutting. Herger responded: "The kingdom of Rothgar has no fighting warriors or earls; they are all long since dead, and we alone must defend the kingdom. Yesterday we were thirteen. Today we are ten, and of that ten two are wounded and cannot fight as full men. The black mist is angered, and it will take a terrible vengeance."

I said to Herger, who had suffered some minor wounds in the fray—but nothing so fierce as the claw marks upon my own face, which I bore proudly—that I feared nothing the demons would do.

He answered curtly that I was an Arab and understood nothing of the ways of the North country, and he told me that the vengeance of the black mist would be terrible and profound. He said, "They will return as Korgon."

I did not know the sense of the word. "What is Korgon?"

He said to me, "The glowworm dragon, which swoops down through the air."

Now this seemed fanciful, but I had already seen the sea monsters just as they said that such beasts truly lived, and also I saw Herger's strained and tired countenance, and I perceived that he believed in the glowworm dragon. I said, "When will Korgon come?"

"Perhaps tonight," Herger said.

Verily, even as he spoke, I saw that Buliwyf, though he had slept not at all during the night and his eyes were red and heavy with fatigue, was directing anew the building of defenses around the hall of Hurot. All the people of the kingdom worked, the children and the women and the old men, and the slaves as well, under the direction of Buliwyf and his lieutenant Ecthgow.

This is what they did: about the perimeter of Hurot and the adjacent buildings, those being the dwellings of the King Rothgar and some of his nobles, and the rude huts of the slaves of these families, and one or another of the farmers who lived closest to the sea, all around this area Buliwyf erected a kind of fence of crossed lances and poles with sharpened points. This fence was not higher than a man's shoulders, and although the points were sharp and menacing, I could not see the value of this defense, for men could scale it easily.

I spoke of this to Herger, who called me a stupid Arab. Herger was in an ill temper.

Now a further defense was constructed, a ditch outside the pole fence, one and a half paces beyond. This ditch was most peculiar. It was not deep, never more than a man's knees, and often less. It was unevenly dug, so that in places it was shallow, and in other places deeper, with small pits. And in places short lances were sunk into the earth, points upward.

I understood the value of this paltry ditch no better than the fence, but I did not inquire of Herger, already knowing his mood. Instead I aided in the work as best I could, pausing only once to have my way with a slavewoman in the Northman's fashion, for in the excitement of the night's battle and the day's preparations I was most energetic.

Now, during my journey with Buliwyf and his warriors

up the Volga, Herger had told me that unknown women, especially if attractive or seductive, were to be mistrusted. Herger said to me that within the forests and wild places of the North country there live women who are called wood-women. These woodwomen entice men by their beauty and soft words, yet when a man approaches them, he finds that they are hollow at the back part, and are apparitions. Then the woodwomen cast a spell upon the seduced man and he becomes their captive.

Now, Herger had thus warned me, and verily it is true that I approached this slavewoman with trepidation, because I did not know her. And I felt her back with my hand, and she laughed; for she knew the reason of the touch, to assure myself that she was no wood spirit. I felt a fool at that time, and cursed myself for placing faith in a heathen superstition. Yet I have discovered that if all those around you believe some particular thing, you will soon be tempted to share in that belief, and so it was with me.

The women of the North people are pale as the men, and equally as tall in stature; the greater number of them looked down upon my head. The women have blue eyes and wear their hair very long, but the hair is fine and easily snarled. Therefore they bundle it up about their necks and upon their heads; to aid in this, they have fashioned for themselves all manner of clasps and pins of ornamented silver or wood. This constitutes their principal adornment. Also the wife of a rich man wears neck chains of gold and silver, as I have earlier said; so, too, do the women favor bracelets of silver, formed in the shape of dragons and snakes, and these they wear upon the arm between the elbow and shoulder. The designs of the North people are intricate and interlaced, as if to portray the weaving of tree branches or serpents; these designs are most beautiful.*

The North people account themselves keen judges of beauty in women. But in truth, all their women seemed to my eyes to be emaciated, their bodies all angles and lumpy with bones; their faces, too, are bony and the cheeks set high. These qualities the Northmen value and praise, although such a woman would not attract a glance in the City of Peace but would be accounted no better than a half-starved dog with protruding ribs. The Northwomen have ribs that protrude in just such a fashion.

I do not know why the women are so thin, for they eat lustily, and as much as the men, yet gain no flesh upon their bodies.

Also the women show no deference, or any demure behavior; they are never veiled, and they relieve themselves in public places, as suits their urge. Similarly they will make bold advances to any man who catches their fancy, as if they were men themselves; and the warriors never chide them for this. Such is the case even if the woman be a slave, for as I have said, the Northmen are most kind and forbearing to their slaves, especially the women slaves.

With the progression of the day, I saw clearly that the

---

* An Arab would be especially inclined to think so, for Islamic religious art tends to be nonrepresentational, and in quality similar to much Scandinavian art, which often seems to favor pure design. However, the Norsemen had no injunction against representing gods, and often did so.

defenses of Buliwyf would not be completed by nightfall, neither the pole fence nor the shallow ditch. Buliwyf saw it also, and called to King Rothgar, who summoned the old crone. This old crone, who was withered and had the beard of a man, killed a sheep and spread the entrails* on the ground. Then she made a variety of chanting song, which lasted a lengthy time, with much supplication to the sky.

I still did not ask Herger of this, because of his mood. Instead I watched the other warriors of Buliwyf, who looked to the sea. The ocean was gray and rough, the sky leaden, but a strong breeze blew toward the land. This satisfied the warriors, and I guessed the reason: that an ocean breeze toward the land would prevent the mist from descending from the hills. This was true.

Upon nightfall, work was halted on the defenses, and to my perplexity Rothgar held another banquet of splendid proportions; and this evening while I watched, Buliwyf, and Herger, and all the other warriors drank much mead and reveled as if they lacked any worldly cares, and had their way with the slavewomen, and then all sank into a stuporous droning sleep.

* أُوْرِدَة : literally, "veins." The Arabic phrase has led to some scholarly errors; E. D. Graham has written, for example, that "the Vikings foretold the future by a ritual of cutting the veins of animals and spreading them on the ground." This is almost certainly wrong; the Arabic phrase for cleaning an animal is "cutting the veins," and Ibn Fadlan was here referring to the widespread practice of divination by examination of entrails. Linguists, who deal with such vernacular phrases all the time, are fond of discrepancies in meaning; a favorite example of Halstead's is the English warning "Look out!" which usually means that one should do exactly the opposite and dive for cover.

Now this also I learned: that each of the warriors of Buliwyf had chosen from among the slavewomen one whom in particular they favored, although not to the exclusion of others. In intoxication, Herger said to me of the woman he had favored, "She shall die with me, if need be." From this I took as the meaning that each of the warriors of Buliwyf had selected some woman who would die for him upon the funeral pyre, and this woman they treated with more courtesy and attention than the others; for they were visitors to this country, and had no slavewomen of their own who could be ordered by kin to do their bidding.

Now, in the early period of my time among the Venden, the Northwomen would not approach me, on account of my darkness of skin and hair, but there was much whispering and glancing in my direction, and giggles one to another. I saw that these unveiled women would nonetheless make a veil with their hands from time to time, and especially when they were laughing. Then I had asked of Herger: "Why do they do this thing?" for I wished not to behave in a manner contrary to the North custom.

Herger made this reply: "The women believe that the Arabs are as stallions, for so they have heard as a rumor." Nor was this any amazement to me, for this reason: in all the lands I have traveled, and so also within the round walls of the City of Peace, verily in every location where men gather and make for themselves a society, I have learned these things to be truths. First, that the peoples of a particular land believe their customs to be fitting and proper and better than any other. Second, that any stranger, a man or also a woman, is accounted inferior in all ways save in the matter of generation. Thus the Turks believe the Persians gifted lovers; the Persians stand in awe of the black-skinned peoples; and they in turn of some others, severally; and so it continues, sometimes by reason given of proportion of genitalia, sometimes by reason given of endurance in the act, sometimes by reason given of especial skill or posturing.

I cannot say whether the Northwomen truly believe as Herger spoke, but verily I discovered that they were much amazed at me by virtue of my surgery,* which practice is unknown among them, as they are dirty heathens. Of the manner of trysting, these women are noisy and energetic, and of such odor that I was obliged to stop my breath for the duration; also they are given to bucking and twisting, scratching and biting, so that a man may be thrown from his mount, as the Northmen speak of it. For myself I accounted the whole business more pain than pleasure.

The Northmen say of the act, "I did battle with such a woman or another," and proudly show their blue marks and abrasions to their comrades, as if these were true wounds of warfare. However, the men never did injury to any woman that I could see.

Now this night, while all the warriors of Buliwyf slept, I was too afraid to drink or laugh; I feared the return of the wendol. Yet they did not return, and I also eventually slept, but fitfully.

Now in the following day there was no wind, and all the

* Circumcision.

people of the kingdom of Rothgar worked with dedication
and fear; there was talk everywhere of the Korgon, and the
certainty that it would attack upon the night. The claw-
mark wounds on my face now pained me, for they pinched
as they healed, and ached whenever I moved my mouth to
eat or speak. Also it is true that my warrior's fever had left
me. I was afraid once more, and I worked in silence alongside the women and old men.

Toward the middle time of the day, I was visited by the
old and toothless noble whom I had spoken to in the banquet hall. This old noble sought me out, and said thus in
Latin, "I will have words with you." He led me to step a
few paces apart from the workers at the defenses.

Now he made a great show of examining my wounds,
which in truth were not serious, and while he examined
these cuts he said to me, "I have a warning for your company. There is unrest in the heart of Rothgar." This he
spoke in Latin.

"What is the cause?" I said.

"It is the herald, and also the son Wiglif, who stands at the
ear of the King," the old nobleman said. "And also the
friend of Wiglif. Wiglif speaks to Rothgar that Buliwyf and
his company plan to kill the King and rule the kingdom."

"That is not the truth," I said, although I did not know
this. In honest fact, I had thought upon this matter from
time to time; Buliwyf was young and vital, and Rothgar
old and weak, and while it is true that the ways of the
Northmen are strange, it is also true that all men are the
same.

"The herald and Wiglif are envious of Buliwyf," the old noble spoke to me. "They poison the air in the ear of the King. All this I tell to you so that you may tell the others to be wary, for this is a matter fit for a basilisk." And then he pronounced my wounds to be minor, and turned away.

Then the noble came back once more. He said, "The friend of Wiglif is Ragnar," and he went away a second time, not looking back upon me further.

In great consternation, I dug and worked at the defenses until I found myself near to Herger. The mood of Herger was still as grim as it had been upon the day previous. He greeted me with these words: "I do not want to hear the questions of a fool."

I said to him that I had no questions, and I reported to him what the old noble had spoken to me; also I told him it was a matter fit for a basilisk.* At my speech, Herger frowned and swore oaths and stamped his foot, and bid me accompany him to Buliwyf.

---

* Ibn Fadlan does not describe a basilisk, apparently assuming that his readers are familiar with the mythological creature, which appears in the early beliefs of nearly all Western cultures. Also known as a cockatrice, the basilisk is generally a variety of cock with a serpent's tail and eight legs, and sometimes bearing scales instead of feathers. What is always true of the basilisk is that his stare is deadly, like the stare of a Gorgon; and the venom of the basilisk is particularly lethal. According to some accounts, a person who stabs a basilisk will watch the venom travel up the sword and onto his hand. The man will then be obliged to cut off his own hand to save his body.

It is probably this sense of the danger of the basilisk that prompts its mention here. The old noble is telling Ibn Fadlan that a direct confrontation with the troublemakers will not solve the problem. Interestingly, one way to dispatch a basilisk was to let it see its reflected image in a mirror; it would then be killed by its own stare.

Buliwyf directed work on the ditch at the other side of the encampment; Herger drew him aside, and spoke rapidly in the Norse tongue, with gestures to my person. Buliwyf frowned, and swore oaths and stamped his foot much as Herger, and then asked a question. Herger said to me, "Buliwyf asks who is the friend of Wiglif? Did the old man tell you who is the friend of Wiglif?"

I responded that he had, and the friend was of the name Ragnar. At this report, Herger and Buliwyf spoke further among themselves, and disputed briefly, and then Buliwyf turned away and left me with Herger. "It is decided," Herger said.

"What is decided?" I inquired.

"Keep your teeth together," Herger said, which is a North expression meaning do not talk.

Thus I returned to my labors, understanding no more than I had at the beginning of the matter. Once again I thought these Northmen to be the most peculiar and contrary men on the face of the earth, for in no matter do they behave as one would expect sensible beings to behave. Yet I worked upon their silly fence, and their shallow ditch; and I watched, and waited.

At the time of the afternoon prayer, I observed that Herger had taken up a work position near to a strapping, giant youth. Herger and this youth toiled side by side in the ditch for some time, and it appeared to my way of seeing that Herger took some pains to fling dirt into the face of the youth, who was in truth a head taller than Herger, and younger, too.

The youth protested, and Herger apologized; but soon

was flinging dirt again. Again, Herger apologized; now the
youth was angry and his face was red. No more than a short
time passed before Herger was again flinging dirt, and the
youth sputtered and spat it and was angry in the extreme.
He shouted at Herger, who later told me the words of their
conversation, although the meaning was evident enough at
the time.

The youth spoke: "You dig as a dog."

Herger spoke in answer: "Do you call me a dog?"

To this, the youth said: "No, I said that you dig as a dog,
flinging* earth carelessly, as an animal."

* ط ْ سَوٌ, ـدـلـح in Arabic, and in the Latin texts, *verbera*. Both words
meaning "flogging" or "whipping," and not "flinging," as this passage is ordinarily translated. It is usually assumed that Ibn Fadlan
used the metaphor of "whipping" with dirt to emphasize the ferocity
of the insult, which is clear enough in any case. However, he may
have consciously or unconsciously transmitted a distinctly Scandinavian attitude toward insults.

Another Arab reporter, al-Tartushi, visited the town of Hedeby in
A.D. 950, and said this about the Scandinavians: "They are most peculiar in the matter of punishment. They have only three penalties for
wrongdoing. The first of these and the most feared is banishment
from the tribe. The second is to be sold into slavery and the third is
death. Women who do wrong are sold as slaves. Men always prefer
death. Flogging is unknown to the Northmen."

This view is not precisely shared by Adam of Bremen, a German
ecclesiastical historian, who wrote in 1075: "If women have been
found unchaste, they are sold off at once, but if men are found guilty
of treason or any other crime, they prefer to be beheaded than
flogged. No form of punishment other than the axe or slavery is
known to them."

The historian Sjögren places great importance on Adam's state-
ment that men would prefer to be beheaded rather than flogged. This
would seem to suggest that flogging was known among the Northmen; and he argues further that it was most likely a punishment for
slaves. "Slaves are property, and it is economically unwise to kill
them for minor offenses; surely whipping was an accepted form of
punishment to a slave. Thus it may be that warriors viewed whipping

Herger spoke: "Do you then call me an animal?"

The youth replied: "You mistake my words."

Now Herger said, "Indeed, for your words are twisted and timid as a feeble old woman."

"This old woman shall see you taste death," the youth said, and drew forth his sword. Then Herger also drew his, for the youth was the same Ragnar, the friend of Wiglif, and thus I saw manifested the intention of Buliwyf in the matter.

These Northmen are most sensitive and touchy about their honor. Among their company, duels occur as frequently as micturition, and a battle to the death is counted ordinary. It may occur on the spot of the insult, or if it is to be formally conducted, the combatants meet at the joining place of three roads. It was thus that Ragnar challenged Herger to fight him.

---

as a degraded penalty because it was reserved for slaves." Sjögren also argues that "all we know of Viking life points to a society founded upon the idea of shame, not guilt, as the negative behavioral pole. Vikings never felt guilt about anything, but they defended their honor fiercely, and would avoid a shameful act at any cost. Passively submitting to the whip must have been adjudged shameful in the extreme, and far worse than death itself."

These speculations carry us back to Ibn Fadlan's manuscript, and his choice of the words "whipping with dirt." Since the Arab is so fastidious, one might wonder whether his words reflect an Islamic attitude. In this regard, we should remember that while Ibn Fadlan's world was certainly divided into clean and dirty things and acts, soil itself was not necessarily dirty. On the contrary, *tayammum,* ablution with dust or sand, is carried out whenever ablution with water is not possible. Thus Ibn Fadlan had no particular abhorrence of soil on one's person; he would have been much more upset if he were asked to drink from a gold cup, which was strictly forbidden.

Now this is the Northman custom: at the appointed time, the friends and kin of the duelers assemble at the place of battle and stretch a hide upon the ground. This they fix with four laurel poles. The battle must be fought upon the hide, each man keeping a foot, or both, on the skin all the while; in this fashion they remain close one to another. The two combatants each arrive with one sword and three shields. If a man's three shields all break, he must fight on without protection, and the battle is to the death.

Such were the rules, chanted by the old crone, the angel of death, at the position of the stretched hide, with all the people of Buliwyf and the people of the kingdom of Rothgar gathered around. I was myself there, not so close to the front, and I marveled that these people should forget the threat of the Korgon which had so terrified them earlier; no one cared anything for aught but the duel.

This was the manner of the duel between Ragnar and Herger. Herger struck the first blow, since he had been challenged, and his sword rang mightily on the shield of Ragnar. I myself had fear for Herger, since this youth was so much larger and stronger than he, and indeed Ragnar's first blow smote Herger's shield from its handgrip, and Herger called for his second shield.

Then the battle was joined, and fiercely. I looked once to Buliwyf, whose face was without expression; and to Wiglif and the herald, on the opposite side, who often looked to Buliwyf while the battle raged.

Herger's second shield was likewise broken, and he called for his third and final shield. Herger was much fatigued, and his face damp and red with exertion; the youth Ragnar appeared easy as he battled, with little exertion.

Then the third shield was broken, and Herger's plight was most desperate, or so it seemed for a fleeting moment. Herger stood with both feet solid on the ground, bent and gasping for his air, and most direly fatigued. Ragnar chose this time to fall upon him. Then Herger side-stepped like the flick of a bird's wings, and the youth Ragnar plunged his sword through empty air. Then, Herger threw his own sword from one hand to the other, for these Northmen can fight as well with either hand, and equally strong. And quickly Herger turned and cut off Ragnar's head from behind with a single blow of his sword.

Verily I saw the blood spurt from the neck of Ragnar and the head flew across the air into the crowd, and I saw with my own eyes that the head struck the ground before the body also struck the ground. Now Herger stepped aside, and then I perceived that the battle had been a sham, for Herger no longer puffed and panted, but stood with no sign of fatigue and no heaving of his chest, and he held his sword lightly, and he looked as if he could kill a dozen such men. And he looked at Wiglif and said, "Honor your friend," meaning to see to the burial.

Herger said to me, as we departed the dueling place, that he had acted a sham so that Wiglif should know the men of Buliwyf were not merely strong and brave warriors, but cunning as well. "This will give him more fear," Herger said, "and he will not dare to speak against us."

I doubted his plan would have this effect, but it is true

that the Northmen prize deceit more than the most deceitful Hazar, indeed more than the most lying Bahrain trader, for whom deceit is a form of art. Cleverness in battle and manly things is accounted a greater virtue than pure strength in warriorship.

Yet Herger was not happy, and I perceived that Buliwyf was not happy, either. As the evening approached, the beginnings of the mist formed in the high inland hills. I believed that they were thinking of the dead Ragnar, who was young and strong and brave, and who would be useful in the coming battle. Herger said as much to me: "A dead man is of no use to anyone."

The attack of
the glowworm dragon
Korgon

Now with the fall of darkness, the mist crept down from the hills, slinking as fingers around the trees, seeping over the green fields toward the hall of Hurot and the waiting warriors of Buliwyf. Here there was no respite in work; from a fresh spring, water was diverted to fill the shallow ditch, and then I understood the sense of the plan, for the water concealed the stakes and deeper holes, and thus the moat was treacherous to any invader.

Further still, the women of Rothgar carried goatskin sacks of water from the well, and doused the fence, and the dwelling, and all the surfaces of the hall of Hurot with water. So, also, the warriors of Buliwyf drenched themselves in their armor with water from the spring. The night was damp cold and, thinking this some heathen ritual, I begged excuses, but to no end: Herger doused me head to foot like the rest. I stood dripping and shivering; in truth I cried aloud at the shock of the cold water, and demanded to know the reason. "The glowworm dragon breathes fire," Herger said to me.

Then he offered me a cup of mead to ease the chill, and I drank this cup of mead without a pause, and was glad for it.

Now the night was fully black, and the warriors of Buliwyf awaited the coming of the dragon Korgon. All eyes were turned toward the hills, now lost in the mist of night. Buliwyf himself strode the length of the fortifications, carrying his great sword Runding, speaking low words of encouragement to his warriors. All waited quietly, save one, the lieutenant Ecthgow. This Ecthgow is a master of the hand axe; he had set up a sturdy post of wood some distance from him, and he practiced the throw of his hand axe to this wooden post, over and again. Indeed, many hand axes had been given him; I counted five or six clipped to his broad belt, and others in his hands, and scattered on the ground about him.

In like manner was Herger stringing and testing with his bow and arrow, and also Skeld, for these were the most skilled in marksmanship of the Northmen warriors. The Northmen arrows have iron points and are most excellently constructed, with shafts straight as a taut line. They have within each village or camp a man who is often crippled or lame,.and he is known as the *almsmann;* he fashions the arrows, and also the bows, for the warriors of the region, and for these alms is paid with gold or shells or, as I have myself seen, with food and meat.*

The bows of the Northmen are near the length of their

---

* This passage is apparently the source of the 1869 comment by the scholarly Rev. Noel Harleigh that "among the barbaric Vikings, morality was so perversely inverted that their sense of alms was the dues paid to weaponsmakers." Harleigh's Victorian assurance exceeded his linguistic knowledge. The Norse word *alm* means elm, the resilient wood from which the Scandinavians made bows and arrows. It is only by chance that this word also has an English meaning. (The English "alms" meaning charitable donations is usually thought to derive from the Greek *eleos,* to pity.)

own bodies, and made of birch. The fashion of shooting is this: the arrow shaft is drawn back to the ear, not to the eye, and thence let fly; and the power is such that the shaft may pass cleanly through the body of a man, and not lodge therein; so also may the shaft penetrate a sheet of wood of the thickness of a man's fist. Verily I have seen such power with an arrow with my own eyes, and I myself tried to wield one of their bows, but discovered it ungainly; for it was too large and resistant to me.

These Northmen are skilled in all the manners of warfare and killing with the several weapons that they prize. They speak of the lines of warfare, which has no sense of arrangements of soldiers; for all to them is the combat of one man to another who is his enemy. The two lines of warfare differ as to the weapon. For the broadsword, which is always swung in an arc and never employed in stabbing, they say: "The sword seeks the breath line," which means to them the neck, and thereby the cutting off of the head from the body. For the spear, the arrow, the hand axe, the dagger, and the other tools of stabbing, they say: "These weapons seek the fat line."* By these words they intend the center part of the

---

* *Linea adeps:* literally, "fat line." Although the anatomical wisdom of the passage has never been questioned by soldiers in the thousand years since—for the midline of the body is where the most vital nerves and vessels are all found—the precise derivation of the term has been mysterious. In this regard, it is interesting to note that one of the Icelandic sagas mentions a wounded warrior in 1030 who pulls an arrow from his chest and sees bits of flesh attached to the point; he then says that he still has fat around his heart. Most scholars agree that this is an ironic comment from a warrior who knows that he has been mortally wounded, and this makes good anatomical sense.

In 1874, the American historian Robert Miller referred to this pas-

body from head to groin; a wound in this center line means to them certain death to their opponent. Also they believe it is foremost to strike the belly for its softness than to strike the chest or head portion.

Verily, Buliwyf and all his company kept watchful vigil that night, and I among them. I experienced much fatigue in this alertness, and soon enough was tired as if I had fought a battle, yet none had occurred. The Northmen were not fatigued, but ready at any moment. It is true that they are the most vigilant persons on the face of all the world, ever prepared for any battle or danger; and they find nothing tiresome in this posture, which for them is ordinary from birth. At all times are they prudent and watchful.

After a time I slept, and Herger woke me thus and brusquely: I felt a great thumping and a whistle of air near my head, and upon the opening of my eyes saw an arrow shivering in the wood at the breadth of a hair from my nose. This arrow Herger had shot, and he and all the other laughed mightily at my discomfiture. To me he said, "If

---

sage of Ibn Fadlan when he said, "Although ferocious warriors, the Vikings had a poor knowledge of physiognomy. Their men were instructed to seek out the vertical midline of the opponent's body, but in doing so, of course, they would miss the heart, positioned as it is in the left chest."

The poor knowledge must be attributed to Miller, and not the Vikings. For the last several hundred years, ordinary Western men have believed the heart to be located in the left chest; Americans put their hands over their hearts when they pledge allegiance to the flag; we have a strong folk tradition of soldiers being saved from death by a Bible carried in the breast pocket that stops the fatal bullet, and so on. In fact, the heart is a midline structure that extends to varying degrees into the left chest; but a midline wound in the chest will always pierce the heart.

you sleep, you will miss the battle." I said in response that that would be no hardship according to my own way of thinking.

Now Herger retrieved his arrow and, observing that I was offended with his prank, sat alongside me and spoke in a manner of friendliness. Herger this night was in a pronounced mood of joking and fun. He shared with me a cup of mead, and spoke thus: "Skeld is bewitched." At this he laughed.

Skeld was not far off, and Herger spoke loudly, so I recognized that Skeld was to overhear us; yet Herger spoke in Latin, unintelligible to Skeld; so perhaps there was some other reason I do not know. Skeld in this time sharpened the points of his arrows and awaited the battle. To Herger I said: "How is he bewitched?"

In reply Herger said: "If he is not bewitched, he may be turning Arab, for he washes his undergarments and also his body each day. Have you not observed this for yourself?"

I answered that I had not. Herger, laughing much, said, "Skeld does this for such and such a freeborn woman, who has captured his fancy. For her he washes each day, and acts a delicate timid fool. Have you not observed this?"

Again I answered that I had not. To this Herger spoke: "What do you see instead?" and laughed much at his own wit, which I did not share, or even pretend, for I was not of a mood to laugh. Now Herger says, "You Arabs are too dour. You grumble all the while. Nothing is laughable to your eyes."

Here I said that he spoke wrongly. He challenged me to

speak a humorous story, and I told him of the sermon of the famous preacher. You know this well. A famous preacher stands in the pulpit of the mosque, and from all around men and women have gathered to hear his noble words. A man, Hamid, puts on a robe and veil and sits among the women. The famous preacher says: "According to Islam, it is desirable that one should not let his or her pubic hair grow too long." A person asks: "How long is too long, O preacher?" All know this story; it is a rude joke, indeed. The preacher replies: "It should not be longer than a barley." Now Hamid asks the woman next to him: "Sister, please check to tell me if my pubic hair is longer than a barley." The woman reaches under Hamid's robes to feel the pubic hair, whereupon her hand touches his organ. In her surprise she utters a cry. The preacher hears this and is much pleased. To the audience he says. "You should all learn the art of attending a sermon, as this lady does, for you can see how it touched her heart." And the woman, still shocked, makes this reply: "It didn't touch my heart, O preacher; it touched my hand."

Herger listened to all my words with a flat countenance. Never did he laugh nor even smile. At my conclusion he said, "What is a preacher?"

To this I said he was a stupid Northman who knew nothing of the wideness of the world. And to this he laughed, whereas he did not laugh at the fable.

Now Skeld gave a shout, and all the warriors of Buliwyf, myself among them, turned to look at the hills, behind the blanket of mist. Here is what I saw: high in the air, a glowing fiery point of light, like a blazing star, and a distance off. All the warriors saw it, and there was murmuring and exclamation among them.

Soon appeared a second point of light, and yet another, and then another. I counted past a dozen and then ceased to count further. These glowing fire-points appeared in a line, which undulated like a snake, or verily like the undulating body of a dragon.

"Be ready now," Herger said to me, and also the Northmen's saying: "Luck in battle." This wish I repeated back to him in the same words, and he moved away.

The glowing fire-points were still distant, yet they came closer. Now I heard a sound which I took as thunder. This was a deep distant rumbling that swelled in the misty air, as all sounds do in mist. For verily it is true that in mist a man's whisper can be heard a hundred paces distant, clear as if he whispered in your own ear.

Now I watched, and listened, and all the warriors of Buliwyf gripped their weapons and watched and listened likewise, and the glowworm dragon of Korgon bore down upon us in thunder and flame. Each blazing point grew larger, and baleful red, flickering and licking; the body of the dragon was long and shimmering, a vision most fierce of aspect, and yet I was not afraid, for I determined now that these were horsemen with torches, and this proved true.

Soon, then, from out of the mist the horsemen emerged, black shapes with raised torches, black steeds hissing and charging, and the battle was joined. Immediately the night air filled with dreadful screams and cries of agony, for the first charge of horsemen had struck the trench, and many mounts tumbled and fell, spilling their riders, and the torches sputtered in the water. Other horses tried to leap the fence, to be impaled on the sharp stakes. A section of the fence caught fire. Warriors ran in all directions.

Now I saw one of the horsemen ride through the burning section of fence, and I could see this wendol clearly for the first time, and verily I saw this: on a black steed rode a human figure in black, but his head was the head of a bear. I was startled with a time of most horrible fright, and I feared I should die from fear alone, for never had I witnessed such a nightmare vision; yet at the same moment the hand axe of Ecthgow was buried deep into the back of the rider, who toppled and fell, and the bear's head rolled from his body, and I saw that he had beneath the head of a man.

Quick as a lightning bolt, Ecthgow leapt upon the fallen creature, stabbed deep into the chest, turned the corpse and withdrew his hand axe from the back, and ran to join the battle. I also joined the battle, for I was knocked spinning from my feet by the blow of a lance. Many riders were now within the fence, their torches blazing; some had the heads of bears and some did not; they circled and tried to set the buildings and the hall of Hurot afire. Against this, Buliwyf and his men battled valiantly.

I came to my feet just as one of the mist monsters bore down upon me with charging steed. Verily I did this: I stood firm my ground and held my lance upward, and the impact I thought would rend me. Yet the lance passed through the body of the rider, and he screamed most horribly, but he did not fall from his mount, and rode on. I fell gasping with pain in my stomach, but I was not truly injured save for the moment.

During the time of this battle, Herger and Skeld loosed their many arrows, and the air was filled with their whistles, and they reached many marks. I saw the arrow of Skeld pass through the neck of one rider, and lodge there; yet again I saw Skeld and Herger both pierce a rider in the chest, and so quickly did they unsheath and draw again that this same rider soon bore four shafts buried in his body, and his screaming was most dreadful as he rode.

Yet I learned this deed was accounted poor fighting by Herger and Skeld, for the Northmen believe that there is nothing sacred in animals; so to them the proper use of arrows is the killing of horses, to dislodge the rider. They say of this: "A man off his horse is half a man, and twice killable." Thus they proceed with no hesitations.*

Now I also saw this: a rider swept into the compound, bent low on his galloping black horse, and he caught up the body of the monster Ecthgow had slain, swung it over his horse's neck, and rode off, for as I have said, these mist monsters leave no dead to be found in the morning light.

The battle raged on a goodly period of time by the light of the blazing fire through the mist. I saw Herger in mortal

---

* According to divine law, Muslims believe that "the Messenger of God has forbidden cruelty to animals." This extends to such mundane details as the commandment to unload pack animals promptly, so that they will not be unnecessarily burdened. Furthermore, the Arabs have always taken a special delight in breeding and training horses. The Scandinavians had no special feeling toward animals; nearly all Arab observers commented on their lack of affection for horses.

combat with one of the demons; taking up a fresh lance, I drove it deep into the creature's back. Herger, dripping blood, raised an arm in thanks and plunged back into the combat. Here I felt great pride.

Now I tried to withdraw my lance, and whilst so doing, was knocked aside by some passing horseman, and from that time in truth I remember little. I saw that one of the dwellings of the nobles of Rothgar was burning in licking spitting flame, but that the doused hall of Hurot was still untouched, and I was glad as if I were myself a Northman, and such were my final thoughts.

Upon the dawn, I was roused by some manner of bathing upon the flesh of my face, and was pleased for the gentle touch. Soon then, I saw that I received the ministrations of a licking dog, and felt much the drunken fool, and was mortified, as may be imagined.*

* Most early translators of Ibn Fadlan's manuscript were Christians with no knowledge of Arabic culture, and their interpretation of this passage reflects that ignorance. In a very free translation, the Italian Lacalla (1847) says: "In the morning I arose from my drunken stupor like a common dog, and was much ashamed for my condition." And Skovmand, in his 1919 commentary, brusquely concludes that "one cannot place credence in Ibn Fadlan's stories, for he was drunk during the battles, and admits as much." More charitably, Du Chatellier, a confirmed Vikingophile, said in 1908: "The Arab soon acquired the intoxication of battle that is the very essence of the Norse heroic spirit."

I am indebted to Massud Farzan, the Sufi scholar, for explaining the allusion that Ibn Fadlan is making here. Actually, he is comparing himself to a character in a very old Arabic joke:

A drunken man falls into a puddle of his own vomit by the roadside. A dog comes along and begins licking his face. The drunk assumes a kind person is cleaning his face, and says gratefully, "May Allah make your children obedient." Then the dog raises his leg

Now I saw that I lay in the ditch, where the water was red as blood itself; I arose and walked through the smoking compound, past all manner of death and destruction. I saw that the earth was soaked in blood, as from a rain, with many puddles. I saw the bodies of slain nobles, and dead women and children likewise. So, also, I saw three or four whose bodies were charred and crusted from fire. All these bodies lay everywhere upon the ground and I was obliged to cast my eyes downward lest I step upon them, so thickly were they spread.

Of the defense works, much of the pole fence had been burned away. Upon other sections, horses lay impaled and cold. Torches were scattered here and there. I saw none of the warriors of Buliwyf.

No cries or mourning came from the kingdom of Rothgar, for the North people do not lament any death, but on the contrary there was unusual stillness in the air. I heard the crowing of a cock, and the bark of a dog, but no human voices in the daylight.

Then I entered the great hall of Hurot, and here found two bodies laid upon the rushes, with their helmets upon their chests. There was Skeld, an earl of Buliwyf; there was Helfdane, earlier injured and now cold and pale. Both were

---

and urinates on the drunkard, who responds, "And may God bless you, brother, for having brought warm water to wash my face."

In Arabic, the joke carries the usual injunction against drunkenness, and the subtle reminder that liquor is *khmer,* or filth, as is urine.

Ibn Fadlan probably expected his reader to think, not that he was ever drunk, but rather that he luckily avoided being urinated upon by the dog, as he earlier escaped death in battle: it is a reference, in other words, to another near miss.

dead. Also there was Rethel, youngest of the warriors, who sat upright in a corner and was attended by slavewomen. Rethel had been wounded previously but he had a fresh injury in his stomach, and there was much blood; surely it pained him greatly, and yet he showed only cheer, and he smiled and teased the slavewomen by the practice of pinching their breasts and buttocks, and often they chided him for causing their distraction as they attempted to bind his wounds.

Here is the manner of the treatment of wounds, according to their nature. If a warrior be wounded in the extremity, either the arm or the leg, a ligature is tied about the extremity, and cloths boiled in water placed over the wound to cover it. Also, I was told that spider webs or bits of lamb's wool may be placed into the wound to thicken the blood and stop its flow; this I never observed.

If a warrior be wounded in the head or the neck, his injury is bathed clean and examined by the slavewomen. If the skin is rent but the white bones whole, then they say of such a wound, "It is no matter." But if the bones are cracked, or broken open in some fashion, then they say, "His life issues out and soon escapes."

If a warrior be wounded in the chest, they feel his hands and feet, and if these are warm, they say of such a wound, "It is no matter." Yet if this warrior coughs or vomits blood, they say, "He speaks in blood," and count this most serious. A man may die of the blood-speaking illness, or he may not, as is his fate.

If a warrior is wounded in the abdomen, they feed him a

soup of onions and herbs; then the women smell about his wounds, and if they smell onions, they say, "He has the soup illness," and they know he shall die.

I saw with my own eyes the women prepare a soup of onion for Rethel, who drank a quantity of this; and the slave-women smelled at his wound, and they smelled the odor of onion. At this, Rethel laughed and made some manner of hearty joke, and called for mead, which was brought him, and he showed no trace of any care.

Now Buliwyf, the leader, and all his warriors conferred in another place in the great hall. I joined their company, but was accorded no greeting. Herger, whose life I had saved, made no notice of me, for the warriors where deep in solemn conversation. I had learned some of the Norse speech, but not sufficient to follow their low and quickly spoken words, and so I walked to another place and drank some mead, and felt the aches of my body. Then a slavewoman came to bathe my wounds. These were a cut in the calf and another on my chest. These injuries I had been insensible to until the time she made offer of her ministrations.

The Northmen bathe wounds with ocean seawater, be-lieving this water to possess more curative powers than spring water. Such bathing with seawater is not agreeable to the wound. In truth I groaned and at this, Rethel laughed and spoke to a slavewoman: "He is still an Arab." Here I was ashamed.

Also the Northmen will bathe wounds in the heated urine of cows. This I refused, when it was offered me.

The North people think cow urine an admirable substance,

and store it up in wooden containers. In the ordinary way of things, they boil it until it is dense and stinging to the nostrils, and then employ this vile liquid for washing, especially of coarse white garments.*

Also I was told that, upon one time or another, the North people may be engaged in a long sea voyage and have at hand no supplies of fresh water, and therefore each man drinks his own urine, and in this way they can survive until they reach shore. This I was told but never saw, by the grace of Allah.

Now Herger came to me, for the conference of the warriors was at an end. The slavewoman attending me had made my wounds burn most distractingly; yet I was determined to maintain a Northman show of great cheer. I said to Herger, "What trifling matter shall we undertake next?"

Herger looked to my wounds, and said to me, "You can ride well enough." I inquired where I would be riding, and in truth at once lost all my good cheer, for I had great weariness, and no strength for aught but resting. Herger said: "Tonight, the glowworm dragon will attack again. But we are now too weak, and our numbers too few. Our defenses are burned and destroyed. The glowworm dragon will kill us all."

These words he spoke calmly. I saw this, and said to Herger: "Where, then, do we ride?" I had in mind that by reason of their heavy losses, Buliwyf and his company might be abandoning the kingdom of Rothgar. In this I was not opposed.

* Urine is a source of ammonia, an excellent cleaning compound.

Herger said to me: "A wolf that lies in its lair never gets meat, or a sleeping man victory." This is a Northman proverb, and from it I took a different plan: that we were going to attack on horseback the mist monsters where they lay, in the mountains or the hills. With no great heart I inquired of Herger when this should be, and Herger told me in the middle part of the day.

Now I saw also that a child entered the hall, and carried in his hands some object of stone. This was examined by Herger, and it was another of the headless stone carvings of a pregnant woman, bloated and ugly. Herger shouted an oath, and dropped the stone from his trembling hands. He called upon the slavewoman, who took the stone and placed it in the fire, where the heat of the flames caused it to crack and splinter into fragments. These fragments were then thrown into the sea, or so I was informed by Herger.

I inquired what was the meaning of the carved stone, and he said to me, "That is the image of the mother of the eaters of the dead, she who presides over them, and directs them in the eating."

Now I saw that Buliwyf, who stood in the center of the great hall, was looking up at the arm of one of the fiends, which still hung from the rafters. Then he looked down at the two bodies of his slain companions, and at the waning Rethel, and his shoulders fell, and his chin sank to his chest. And then he walked past them and out of the door, and I saw him put on his armor, and take up his sword, and prepare for battle anew.

The desert of dread

Buliwyf called for seven sturdy horses, and in the early part of the day we rode from the great hall of Rothgar out into the flat plain, and thence toward the hills beyond. With us also were four hounds of pure white color, great animals which I should count nearer to wolves than dogs, so fierce was their demeanor. This made the totality of our attacking forces, and I believed it a weak gesture against so formidable an opponent, yet the Northmen place great faith upon surprise and a sly attack. Also, by their own reckoning they are each man the equal of three or four of any other.

I was not disposed to embark upon another venture of warfare, and was much amazed that the Northmen did not reflect such a view, springing as it did from the fatigue of my body. Herger said of this: "It is always thus, now and in Valhalla," which is their idea of heaven. In this heaven, which is to them a great hall, warriors battle from dawn to dusk; then those who are dead are revived, and all share a feast in the night, with endless food and drink; and then upon the day they battle again; and those who die are revived, and there is a feast; and this is the nature of their heaven through all eternity.* Thus they never count it strange to do battle day upon day while on the earth.

Our direction of travel was determined by the trail of blood the retreating horsemen had left from the night. The hounds led, racing along this red dripping trail. We paused but once upon the flat plain, to retrieve a weapon dropped by the departing demons. Here is the nature of the weapon: it was a hand axe with a haft of some wood, and a blade of chipped stone bound to the haft with hide thongs. The edge of this axe was exceedingly sharp, and the blade fashioned with skill, as much as if this stone were some gemstone to be chiseled to delight a rich lady's vanity. Such was the degree of workmanship, and the weapon was formidable for the sharpness of its edge. Never have I seen such an object before on the face of all the earth. Herger told me that the wendol made all their tools and weapons of this stone, or so the Northmen believe.

Yet we traveled onward with good speed, led by the barking dogs, and their barking cheered me. At length we came to the hills. We rode into the hills without hesitation or ceremony, each of the warriors of Buliwyf intent upon his purpose, a silent and grim-faced company of men. They held the marks of fear upon their faces, and yet no man paused or faltered, but pressed onward.

---

* Some authorities on mythology argue that the Scandinavians did not originate this idea of an eternal battle, but rather that this is a Celtic concept. Whatever the truth, it is perfectly reasonable that Ibn Fadlan's companions should have adopted the concept, for the Scandinavians had been in contact with Celts for over a hundred and fifty years at this time.

Now it was cold in the hills, in the forests of dark green trees, and a chill wind blew at our clothing, and we saw the hissing breath of the steeds, and white plumes of breath from the running dogs, and we pressed onward still. After some travel until the middle period of the day, we arrived at a new landscape. Here was a brackish tarn, or moor, or heath —a desolate land, most resembling a desert, yet not sandy and dry, but damp and soggy, and over this land lay the faintest wisps of mist. The Northmen call this place the desert of dread.*

Now I saw with my own eyes that this mist lay upon the land in small pockets or clusterings, like tiny clouds seated upon the earth. In one area, the air is clear; then in another place there are small mists that hang near the ground, rising to the height of a horse's knees, and in such a place we would lose sight of the dogs, who were enveloped in these mists. Then, a moment later, the mist would clear, and we would be in another open space again. Such was the landscape of the heath.

I found this sight remarkable, but the Northmen took it to be nothing special; they said the land in this region has many brackish pools and bubbling hot springs, which rise

---

* صَحرآ٬ خَـوف : literally, "desert of dread." In a paper in 1927, J.G. Tomlinson pointed out that precisely the same phrase appears in the *Völsunga Saga,* and therefore argued at length that it represented a generic term for taboo lands. Tomlinson was apparently unaware that the *Völsunga Saga* says nothing of the sort; the nineteenth-century translation of William Morris indeed contains the line "There is a desert of dread in the uttermost part of the world," but this line was Morris's own invention, appearing in one of the many passages where he expanded upon the original Germanic saga.

from rents in the ground; in these places, a small fog collects, and remains there all the day and night. They call this the place of steaming lakes.

The land is difficult for horses, and we made slower progress. The dogs also ventured more slowly, and I noted that they barked less vigorously. Soon our company had changed wholly: from a gallop, with yelping dogs in the forefront, to a slow walk, with silent dogs hardly willing to lead the way, and instead falling back until they were underfoot the horses, thus causing some occasional difficulty. It was still very cold, indeed colder than before, and I saw here and there a small patch of snow upon the ground, though this was, by my best reckoning, the summer period.

At a slow pace, we proceeded for a goodly distance, and I had wonder that we should be lost, and never find our way back through this heath. Now at a place the dogs halted. There was no difference in the terrain, or any mark or object upon the ground; yet the dogs stopped as if they had arrived upon some fence or palpable obstruction. Our party halted at this place, and looked about in this direction and that. There was no wind, and no sounds were here; not the sound of birds or of any living animal, but only silence.

Buliwyf said, "Here begins the land of the wendol," and the warriors patted their steeds upon the necks to comfort them, for the horses were skittish and nervous in this region. So also were their riders. Buliwyf kept his lips tight; Ecthgow's hands trembled as he held the reins of his horse; Herger was gone quite pale, and his eyes darted to this way and that; so also the others in their way.

The Northmen say, "Fear has a white mouth," and now I saw that this is true, for they were all pale around the lips and mouth. No man spoke of his fear.

Now we left the dogs behind, and rode onward into more snow, which was thin and crunching underfoot, and into thicker mists. No man spoke, save to the horses. At each step these beasts were more difficult to prod onward; the warriors were obliged to urge them with soft words and sharp kicks. Soon we saw shadowy forms in the mist ahead of us, which we approached with caution. Now I saw with my own eyes this: on either side of the path, mounted high on stout poles, were the skulls of enormous beasts, their jaws opened in a posture of attack. We continued, and I saw these were the skulls of giant bears, which the wendol worship. Herger said to me that the bear skulls protect the borders of the land of the wendol.

Now we sighted another obstacle, gray and distant and large. Here was a giant rock, as high as a horse's saddle, and it was carved in the shape of a pregnant woman, with bulging belly and breasts, and no head or arms or legs. This rock was spattered with the blood of some sacrifices; verily it dripped with streaks of red, and was gruesome to look upon.

No man spoke of what was observed. We rode on apace. The warriors drew out their swords and held them in readiness. Now here is a quality to the Northmen: that previously they showed fear, but having entered into the land of the wendol, close to the source of the fear, their own apprehensions disappeared. Thus do they seem to do all things backward, and in perplexing manner, for verily they now appeared at ease. It was only the horses that were ever more difficult to prod onward.

I smelled, now, the rotting-carcass odor that I had smelled before in the great hall of Rothgar; and as it reached my nostrils anew, I was faint of heart. Herger rode alongside me and said in a soft voice, "How do you fare?"

Not being capable of concealing my emotion, I said to him, "I am afraid."

Herger replied to me: "That is because you think upon what is to come, and imagine fearsome things that would stop the blood of any man. Do not think ahead, and be cheerful by knowing that no man lives forever."

I saw the truth of his words. "In my society," I said, "we have a saying which is: 'Thank Allah, for in his wisdom he put death at the end of life, and not at the beginning.'"

Herger smiled at this, and laughed briefly. "In fear, even Arabs speak the truth," he said, and then rode forward to tell my words to Buliwyf, who also laughed. The warriors of Buliwyf were glad for a joke at that time.

Now we came to a hill and, reaching the crest, paused and looked down upon the encampment of the wendol. Here is how it lay before us, as I saw with my own eyes: there was a valley, and in the valley a circle of rude huts of mud and straw, of poor construction as a child might erect; and in the center of the circle a large fire, now smoldering. Yet there were no horses, no animals, no movement, no sign of life of any kind; and this we saw through the shifting gauze of the mist.

Buliwyf dismounted his steed, and the warriors did like-

wise, myself among them. In truth, my heart pounded and I
was short of breath as I looked down at the savage encampment of the demons. We spoke in whispers. "Why is there
no activity?" I inquired.

"The wendol are creatures of the night even as owls or
bats," Herger replied, "and they sleep during the hours of
the day. So are they sleeping now, and we shall descend into
their company, and fall upon them, and slay them in their
dreams."

"We are so few," I said, for there were many huts below
which I perceived.

"We are enough," Herger said, and then he gave me a
draught of mead, which I drank gratefully, with praise to
Allah that it is not forbidden, or even disapproved of.* In
truth, I was finding my tongue hospitable to this very substance I once thought vile; thus do strange things cease to be
strange upon repetition. In like fashion, I no longer attended
the hideous stench of the wendol, for I had been smelling it
a goodly time and I no longer was aware of the odor.

The North people are most peculiar in the matter of smelling. They are not clean, as I have said; and they eat all manner of evil food and drink; and yet it is true that they value
the nose above all parts of the body. In battle, the loss of an
ear is no great matter; the loss of a finger or toe or a hand
little more; and such scars and injuries they bear indiffer-
ently. But the loss of a nose they count equal to death itself,

* The Islamic injunction against alcohol is literally an injunction
against the fermented fruit of the grape; i.e., wine. Fermented drinks
of honey are specifically permitted to Muslims.

and this even to the loss of a piece of the fleshy tip, which other peoples would say is a most minor injury.

The breaking of the bones of the nose, through battle and blows, is no matter; many of them have crooked noses for that cause. I do not know the reason for this fear of cutting the nose.*

Fortified, the warriors of Buliwyf and I among them left our steeds upon the hill, but these animals could not go unattended, so affrighted were they. One of our party was to remain with them, and I had hopes to be selected to this task; yet it was Haltaf, he being already injured and of least use. Thus we others warily descended the hill among the sickly scrub and dying bushes down the slope to the encampment of the wendol. We moved in stealth, and no alarm was raised, and soon we were in the very heart of the village of the demons.

Buliwyf never spoke, but gave all directions and orders with his hands. And from him I took the meaning that we were to go in groups of two warriors, each pair in a different direction. Herger and I were to attack the nearest of the mud

* The usual psychiatric explanation for such fears of loss of body parts is that they represent castration anxiety. In a 1937 review, *Deformations of Body Image in Primitive Societies,* Engelhardt observes that many cultures are explicit about this belief. For example, the Nanamani of Brazil punish sexual offenders by cutting off the left ear; this is thought to reduce sexual potency. Other societies attach significance to the loss of fingers, toes, or, in the case of the Northmen, the nose. It is a common superstition in many societies that the size of a man's nose reflects the size of his penis.

Emerson argues that the importance accorded the nose by primitive societies reflects a vestigial attitude from the days when men were hunters and relied heavily upon a sense of smell to find game and avoid enemies; in such a life, the loss of smell was a serious injury indeed.

huts, and the others were to attack others. All waited until the groups were stationed outside the huts, and then, with a howl, Buliwyf raised his great sword Runding and led the attack.

I dashed with Herger into one of the huts, blood pounding in my head, my sword light as a feather in my hands. Verily I was ready for the mightiest battle of my life. I saw nothing inside; the hut was deserted and barren as well, save for rude beds of straw, so clumsy in their appearance they seemed more to resemble nests of some animal.

We dashed outside, and attacked the next of these mud huts. Again we found it empty. Verily, all the huts were empty, and the warriors of Buliwyf were sorely vexed and stared one to the next with expression of surprise and astonishment.

Then Ecthgow called to us, and we gathered at one of these huts, larger than any of the others. And here I saw that it was deserted as they were all deserted, but the interior was not barren. Rather, the floor of the hut was littered with fragile bones, which crunched underfoot like the bones of birds, delicate and frail. I was much surprised at this, and stooped to see the nature of these bones. With a shock, I saw the curved line of an eye socket here, and a few teeth there. Verily we stood upon a carpet of the bones of human faces, and for further proofs of this ghastly truth, piled high upon one wall of the hut were the head portions of the human skulls, stacked inverted like so many pottery bowls, but glistening white. I was sick, and departed the hut to purge myself. Herger said to me that the wendol eat the brains of their victims, as a human person might eat eggs or cheese.

Eaters of the Dead

This is their custom; vile as it is to contemplate such a matter, yet it is true.

Now another of the warriors called to us, and we entered another hut. Here I saw this: the hut was bare, except for a large thronelike chair, carved of a single piece of enormous wood. This chair had a high fanning back, carved into the shape of snakes and demons. At the foot of the chair were littered bones of skulls, and upon the arms of the chair, where its owner might rest his hands, there was blood and remnants of whitish cheesy substance, which was human brain material. The odor of this room was ghastly.

Placed all around this chair there were small pregnant stone carvings, such as I have described before; these carvings formed a circle or perimeter about the chair.

Herger said, "This is where she rules," and his voice was low and awed.

I was not able to comprehend his meaning, and was sick in heart and stomach. I emptied my stomach upon the soil. Herger and Buliwyf and the others were also distressed, though no man purged himself, but rather they took glowing embers from the fire and set the huts aflame. They burned slowly, for they were damp.

And thus we climbed up the hill, mounted our horses, and left the region of the wendol, and departed the desert of dread. And all the warriors of Buliwyf were now sad of aspect, for the wendol had surpassed them in cunning and cleverness, abandoning their lair in anticipation of the attack, and they would count the burning of their dwellings no great loss.

The counsel of the dwarf

We returned as we had come, but rode with greater speed for the horses now were eager, and eventually came down from the hills and saw the flat plain and, in the distance, at the ocean's edge, the settlement and the great hall of Rothgar.

Now Buliwyf veered away and led us in another direction, toward high rocky crags swept by the ocean winds. I rode alongside Herger and inquired the reason for this, and he said we were to seek out the dwarves of the region.

At this I was much surprised, for the men of the North have no dwarves among their society; they are never seen in the streets, nor do any sit at the feet of kings, nor are any to be found counting money or keeping records or any of the things that we know of dwarves.* Never had any Northman mentioned dwarves to me, and I had presumed that so giant a people† would never produce dwarves.

---

* In the Mediterranean, from Egyptian times, dwarves were thought especially intelligent and trustworthy, and tasks of bookkeeping and money-handling were reserved to them.

† Of approximately ninety skeletons that can be confidently ascribed to the Viking period in Scandinavia, the average height appears to be about 170 centimeters (5′7″).

Now we came to a region of caves, hollowed and wind-swept, and Buliwyf dismounted from his horse, and all the warriors of Buliwyf did likewise, and proceeded by foot. I heard a hissing sound, and verily I saw puffs of steam issue from one and another of these several caves. We entered one cave and there found dwarves.

They were in appearance thus: of the ordinary size of dwarf, but distinguished by heads of great size, and bearing features that appeared exceedingly aged. There were both male and female dwarves and all had the appearance of great age. The males were bearded and solemn; the women also had some hair upon the face, so they appeared manlike. Each dwarf wore a garment of fur or sable; each also wore a thin belt of hide decorated with bits of hammered gold.

The dwarves greeted our arrival politely, with no sign of fear. Herger said these creatures have magic powers and need fear no man on earth; however, they are apprehensive of horses, and for this reason we had left the mounts behind us. Herger said also that the powers of a dwarf reside in his thin belt, and that a dwarf will do anything to retrieve his belt if it is lost.

Herger said this also: that the appearance of great age among the dwarves was a true thing, and that a dwarf lived beyond the span of any ordinary man. Also he said to me that these dwarves are virile from their earliest youth; that even as infants they have hair at the groin, and members of uncommon size. Indeed, it is in this way that the parents first come to know that their infant child is a dwarf, and a creature of magic, who must be taken to the hills to live with others of his kind. This done, the parents give thanks to the gods and sacrifice some animal or other, for to give birth to a dwarf is accounted high good fortune.

This is the belief of the North people, as Herger spoke it, and I do not know the truth of the matter, and report only what was told to me.

Now I saw that the hissing and steam issued from great cauldrons, into which hammered-steel blades were plunged to temper the metal, for the dwarves make weapons that are highly prized by the Northmen. Indeed, I saw the warriors of Buliwyf looking about the caves eagerly, as any woman in a bazaar shop selling precious silks.

Buliwyf made inquiries of these creatures, and was directed to the topmost of the caves, wherein sat a single dwarf, older than all the others, with a beard and hair of purest white, and a creased and wrinkled face. This dwarf was called "tengol," which means a judge of good and evil, and also a soothsayer.

This tengol must have had the magical powers that all said he did, for he immediately greeted Buliwyf by his name, and bade him sit with him. Buliwyf sat, and we gathered a short distance away, standing.

Now Buliwyf did not present the tengol with gifts; the Northmen make no obeisance to the little people: they believe that the favors of the dwarves must be freely given, and it is wrong to encourage the favors of a dwarf with gifts. Thus Buliwyf sat, and the tengol looked at him, and then closed his eyes and began to speak, rocking back and forth as he sat. The tengol spoke in a high voice as a child, and Herger told me the meaning was thus:

"O Buliwyf, you are a great warrior but you have met your match in the monsters of the mist, the eaters of the dead. This shall be a struggle to the death, and you shall need all your strength and wisdom to overcome the challenge." And he went on in this manner for some good time, rocking back and forth. The import was that Buliwyf faced a difficult adversary, which I already knew well enough and so did Buliwyf himself. Yet Buliwyf was patient.

Also I saw that Buliwyf took no offense when the dwarf laughed at him, which frequently he did. The dwarf spoke: "You have come to me because you attacked the monsters in the brackish marsh and tarn, and this availed you nothing. Therefore you come to me for advice and admonishment, as a child to his father, saying what shall I do now, for all my plans have failed me." The tengol laughed long at this speech. Then his old face turned solemn.

"O Buliwyf," he said, "I see the future, but I can tell you no more than you already know. You and all your brave warriors gathered your skill and your courage to make an attack upon the monsters in the desert of dread. In this you cheated yourself, for such was not a true hero's enterprise."

I heard these words with astonishment, for it had seemed heroic work enough for me.

"No, no, noble Buliwyf," the tengol said. "You set out upon a false mission, and deep in your hero's heart you knew it was unworthy. So, too, was your battle against the glow-worm dragon Korgon unworthy, and it cost you many fine warriors. To what end are all your plans?"

Still Buliwyf did not answer. He sat with the dwarf and waited.

"A hero's great challenge," the dwarf said, "is in the heart, and not in the adversary. What matter if you had come upon the wendol in their lair and had killed many of their number as they slept? You could kill many, yet this would not end the struggle, any more than cutting off the fingers will kill the man. To kill the man, you must pierce the head or the heart, and thus it is with the wendol. All this you know, and need not my counsel to know it."

Thus the dwarf, rocking back and forth, chastised Buliwyf. And thus Buliwyf accepted his rebuke, for he did not reply, but only lowered his head.

"You have done the work of a mere man," the tengol continued, "and not a proper hero. A hero does what no man dares to undertake. To kill the wendol, you must strike at the head and the heart: you must overcome their very mother, in the thunder caves."

I did not understand the meaning of these words.

"You know of this, for it has always been true, through all the ages of man. Shall your brave warriors die, one by one? Or shall you strike at the mother in the caves? Here is no prophecy, only the choice of a man or a hero."

Now Buliwyf made some response, but it was low, and lost to me in the howl of the wind that raked the entrance to the cave. Whatever the words, the dwarf spoke further:

"That is the hero's answer, Buliwyf, and I would expect none other from you. Thus shall I help your quest." Then a number of this kind came forward into the light from the dark recesses of the cave. And they bore many objects.

"Here," said the tengol, "are lengths of rope, made from the skin of seals caught at the first melting of the ice. These ropes will help you to attain the ocean entrance to the thunder caves."

"I thank you," Buliwyf said.

"And here also," the tengol said, "are seven daggers, forged with steam and magic, for you and your warriors. Great swords will be of no avail in the thunder caves. Carry these new weapons bravely, and you shall accomplish all you desire."

Buliwyf took the daggers, and thanked the dwarf. He stood. "When shall we do this thing?" he asked.

"Yesterday is better than today," the tengol replied, "and tomorrow is better than the day which follows that. So make haste, and carry out your intentions with a firm heart and a strong arm."

"And what follows if we succeed?" Buliwyf asked.

"Then the wendol shall be mortally wounded, and thrash in its death throes a final time, and after this last agony the land shall have peace and sunlight forevermore. And your name shall be sung glorious in all the halls of the Northlands, forevermore."

"The deeds of dead men are so sung," Buliwyf said.

"That is true," the dwarf said, and laughed again, the giggle of a child or a young girl. "And also the deeds of heroes who live, but never are sung the deeds of ordinary men. All this you know."

Now Buliwyf departed from the cave, and gave to each of us the dagger of the dwarves, and we descended from the rocky windswept crags, and returned to the kingdom and the great hall of Rothgar as night was falling.

All these things took place, and I saw them with my own eyes.

The events of
the night before the attack

No mist came that night; the fog descended from the hills but hung back among the trees, and did not creep out onto the plain. In the great hall of Rothgar, a mighty feast was held, and Buliwyf and all his warriors joined in great celebration. Two great horned sheep* were slaughtered and consumed; each man drank vast quantities of mead; Buliwyf himself ravished half a dozen slave girls, and perhaps more; but despite this merrymaking neither he nor his warriors were truly cheerful. From one time to another, I saw them glance at the ropes of sealskin and the dwarf daggers, which had been set apart to one side.

Now I joined in the general revelry, for I felt as one of them, having spent much time in their company, or so it seemed. Indeed, that night I felt I had been born a Northman.

Herger, much intoxicated, told me freely of the mother of the wendol. He said this: "The mother of the wendol is very old and she lives in the caves of thunder. These thunder caves

---

*Dahlmann (1924) writes that "for ceremonial occasions the ram was eaten to increase potency, since the horned male animal was judged superior to the female." In fact, during this period both rams and ewes had horns.

lie in the rock of cliffs, not far from here. The caves have two openings, one from the land and another from the sea. But the entrance from the land is guarded by the wendol, who protect their old mother; so it is that we cannot attack from the side of the land, for in this way we would all be killed. Therefore we shall attack from the sea."

I inquired of him: "What is the nature of this mother of the wendol?"

Herger said that no Northman knew this thing, but that it was said among them that she was old, older than the old crone they call the angel of death; and also that she was frightful to look upon; and also that she wore snakes upon her head as a wreath; and also, too, that she was strong beyond all accounting. And he said at the last that the wendol called upon her to direct them in all their affairs of life.* Then Herger turned from me and slept.

*Joseph Cantrell observes that "there is a strain in Germanic and Norse mythology which holds that women have special powers, qualities of magic, and should be feared and mistrusted by men. The principal gods are all men, but the Valkyries, which means literally 'choosers of the slain,' are women who transport dead warriors to Paradise. It was believed that there were three Valkyries, as there were three Norns, or Fates, which were present at the birth of every man, and determined the outcome of his life. The Norns were named Urth, the past; Verthandi, the present; and Skuld, the future. The Norns 'wove' a man's fate, and weaving was a woman's work; in popular representations they were shown as young maidens. Wyrd, an Anglo-Saxon deity which ruled fate, was also a goddess. Presumably the association of women with man's fate was a permutation of earlier concepts of women as fertility symbols; the goddesses of fertility controlled the growing and flowering of crops and living things on the earth."

Cantrell also notes that "in practice, we know that divination, spell-casting, and other shamanistic functions were reserved to elderly women in Norse society. Furthermore, popular ideas of women con-

Now this event occurred: in the depths of the night, as the celebrations were drawing to a close and the warriors were drifting into sleep, Buliwyf sought me out. He sat beside me and drank mead from a horned cup. He was not intoxicated, I saw, and he spoke slowly in the North tongue, so that I should understand his meaning.

He said first to me: "Did you comprehend the words of the dwarf tengol?"

I replied that I did, with the help of Herger, who now snored near to us.

Buliwyf said to me: "Then you know I shall die." He spoke thus, with his eyes clear and his gaze firm. I did not know any reply, or response to make, but finally said to him in the North fashion, "Believe no prophecy until it bears fruit."*

---

tained a heavy element of suspicion. According to the *Havamal*, 'No one should trust the words of a girl or a married woman, for their hearts have been shaped on a turning wheel and they are inconstant by nature.' "

Bendixon says, "Among the early Scandinavians there was a kind of division of power according to sex. Men ruled physical affairs; women, psychological matters."

* This is a paraphrase of a sentiment among the Northmen, expressed fully as: "Praise not the day until evening has come; a woman until she is burnt; a sword until it is tried; a maiden until she is married; ice until it has been crossed; beer until it has been drunk." This prudent, realistic, and somewhat cynical view of human nature and the world was something the Scandinavians and the Arabs shared. And like the Scandinavians, the Arabs often express it in mundane or satiric terms. There is a Sufi story about a man who asked a sage: "Suppose I am traveling in the countryside and must make ablutions in the stream. Which direction do I face while performing the ritual?" To this the sage replies: "In the direction of your clothes, so they won't be stolen."

Buliwyf said: "You have seen much of our ways. Tell me what is true. Do you draw sounds?" I answered that I did. "Then look to your safety, and do not be overbrave. You dress and now you speak as a Northman, and not a foreign man. See that you live."

I placed my hand upon his shoulder, as I had seen his fellow warriors do to him in greeting. He smiled then. "I fear no thing," he said, "and need no comfort. I tell you to look to your own safety, for your own account. Now it is wisest to sleep."

So speaking, he turned away from me, and devoted his attention to a slave girl, whom he pleasured not a dozen paces from where I sat, and I turned away hearing the moans and laughter of this woman. And at length I fell into a sleep.

The thunder caves

Before the first pink streaks of dawn lighted the sky, Buliwyf and his warriors, myself among them, rode out from the kingdom of Rothgar and followed the cliff edge above the sea. On this day I did not feel fit, for my head ached; also was my stomach sour from the celebration of the previous night. Surely all the warriors of Buliwyf were in like condition, yet no man gave signal of these discomforts. We rode briskly, skirting the border of the cliffs which on all this coast are high and forbidding, and sheer; in a sheet of gray stone they drop to the foaming and turbulent sea below. In some places along this coastline there are rocky beaches, but often the land and the sea meet directly, and the waves crash like thunder upon the rocks; and this was the circumstance for the most part.

I saw Herger, who carried upon his horse the sealskin ropes of the dwarves, and I rode up to travel alongside him. I inquired what was our purpose on this day. In truth, I did not care greatly, so badly did my head ache and my stomach burn.

Herger said to me, "On this morning, we attack the mother of the wendol in the thunder caves. This we shall do by attacking from the sea, as I have told you yesterday."

While I rode, I looked from my horse down at the sea, which smashed upon the rock cliffs. "Do we attack by boat?" I inquired of Herger.

"No," Herger said, and slapped his hand upon the seal-skin ropes.

Then I took his meaning to be that we should climb down the cliffs on the ropes, and thereby in some fashion make an entrance into the caves. I was much frightened at this prospect, for never have I liked to be exposed upon high places; even high buildings in the City of Peace have I avoided. I said as much.

Herger said to me, "Be thankful, for you are fortunate."

I inquired the source of my fortune. Herger said in reply, "If you have the fear of high places, then this day you shall overcome it; and so you shall have faced a great challenge; and so you shall be adjudged a hero."

I said to him, "I do not want to be a hero."

At this he laughed and said that I expressed such an opinion only because I was an Arab. Then also he said that I had a stiff head, by which the Northmen mean the after-math of drinking. This was true, as I have already told.

Also it is true that I was much aggrieved at the prospect of climbing down the cliff. Verily I felt in this manner: that I should rather do any action upon the face of the earth, whether to lie with a woman in menses, to drink from a gold cup, to eat the excrement of a pig, to put out my eyes, even to die itself—any or all of these things should I prefer to the climbing of that accursed cliff. Also I was in ill temper.

To Herger I said, "You and Buliwyf and all your company may be heroes as suits your temper, but I have no part in this affair, and shall not number as one of you."

At this speech, Herger laughed. Then he called to Buliwyf, and spoke a rapid speech; Buliwyf answered him back, over his shoulder. Then Herger spoke to me: "Buliwyf says that you will do as we do."

In truth, now I sank into despairing, and said to Herger, "I cannot do this thing. If you force me to do it, I shall surely die."

Herger said, "How shall you die?"

I said to him, "I shall lose my grip from the ropes."

This answer made Herger laugh heartily yet again, and he repeated my words to all the Northmen, and they all laughed at what I had said. Then Buliwyf spoke a few words.

Herger said to me: "Buliwyf says that you shall lose your grip only if you release the ropes from your hands, and only a fool would do such a thing. Buliwyf says you are an Arab, but no fool."

Now, here is a true aspect of the nature of men: that in his fashion Buliwyf said that I could climb the ropes; and that for his speech, I believed it as much as he, and was cheered in my heart to a slight degree. This Herger saw, and he spoke these words: "Each person bears a fear which is special to him. One man fears a close space and another man fears drowning; each laughs at the other and calls him stupid. Thus fear is only a preference, to be counted the same as the preference for one woman or another, or mutton for pig, or cabbage for onion. We say, fear is fear."

I was not in a mood for his philosophies; this I expressed to him, for in truth I was growing closer to anger than to fear. Now Herger laughed at my face and spoke these words: "Praise Allah, for he put death at the end of life, and not at the beginning."

Curtly, I said in reply that I saw no benefit in hastening the end. "Indeed, no man does," Herger responded to me, and then he said, "Look to Buliwyf. See how he sits straight. See how he rides forward, though he knows he shall soon die."

I answered, "I do not know he shall die."

"Yes," Herger said, "but Buliwyf knows." Then Herger spoke nothing further to me, and we rode onward for a goodly period of time, until the sun was high and bright in the sky. Then at last Buliwyf gave the signal to halt, and all the horsemen dismounted, and prepared to enter the thunder caves.

Now, well I knew that these Northmen are brave to a fault, but as I looked at the precipice of the cliff below us, my heart twisted over inside my chest, and I thought I should be purging myself at any instant. Verily, the cliff was absolutely sheer, lacking the least grip for hand or feet, and it descended for the distance of perhaps four hundred paces. Verily, the crashing waves were so far beneath us that they appeared as miniature waves, tiny as the most delicate drawing of an artist. Yet I knew them to be large as any waves on earth, once one descended to that level far below.

To me, the climbing down of these cliffs was madness beyond the madness of a foaming dog. But the Northmen proceeded in normal fashion. Buliwyf directed the pounding of stout wooden stakes into the earth; around these the seal-skin ropes were bound, and the trailing ends flung over the sides of the cliffs.

Verily, the ropes were not long enough for so distant a descent, and thus had to be hauled up again, and two ropes fastened together to make a single length to reach the waves at the bottom.

In due time, we had two such ropes that reached down the side of the cliff face. Then Buliwyf spoke to his gathering: "First I shall proceed, so that when I reach the bottom all shall know that the ropes are stout and the journey can be accomplished. I await you at the bottom, on the narrow ledge you see below."

I looked to this narrow ledge. To call it narrow is to call a camel kind. It was, in truth, the barest strip of flat rock, continually washed and pounded by the surf.

"When all have reached the bottom," Buliwyf said, "we can attack the mother of the wendol in the thunder caves." Thus he spoke, in a voice as ordinary as that which he would command a slave in the preparation of some ordinary stew or any other household chore. And without further speech, he went over the side of the cliff.

Now, here is the manner of his descent, which I found remarkable, but the Northmen account it no particular thing. Herger told to me they use this method for gathering of sea-bird eggs at certain times of the year, when the sea birds build their nests on the cliff face. It is done in this fashion: a sling is placed around the waist of the descending man, and all the fellows strain to lower him down the cliff.

Meanwhile, this same man grips, for support, on to the second rope, which dangles on the cliff face. Further, the descending man carries a stout staff of oaken wood, fitted at one end with a leather thong, or strap, about his wrist; this staff he employs for a prod to push himself hither and yon as he moves down the rocky surface.*

As Buliwyf went down, becoming ever smaller to my eyes, I saw that he maneuvered with the sling, the rope, and the stick very agilely; but I was not deceived into thinking this some trivial matter, for I saw it to be difficult and requiring practice.

At length, he safely reached the bottom and stood on the narrow ledge with the surf crashing over him. In truth, he was so diminished we could hardly see him wave his hand, in signal that he was safe. Now the sling was hauled up; and also with it, the oaken staff. Herger turned to me, speaking: "You shall go next."

I said that I was feeling poorly. Also I said I wished to see another man descend, in order better to study the manner of the descent.

Herger said, "It is more difficult with each descent, because there are fewer here above to lower a man down. The last man must descend without the sling at all, and that shall be Ecthgow, for his arms are iron. It is a mark of our favor which allows you to be the second man to descend. Go now."

I saw in his eyes that there was no hope of delay, and so

---

* In the Faeroe Islands of Denmark, a similar method of scaling cliffs is still practiced to gather bird eggs, an important source of food to the islanders.

I was myself fitted into the sling, and I gripped the stout staff in my hands, which were slippery with sweat; and my whole body likewise was slippery with sweat; and I shivered in the wind as I went over the side of the cliff, and for the last time saw the five Northmen straining at the rope, and then they were lost from view. I made my descent.

I had in my mind to make many prayers to Allah, and also to record in the eye of my mind, in the memory of my soul, the many experiences that a man must undergo as he dangles from ropes down such a wind-torn rocky cliff. Once out of sight of my Northmen friends above, I forgot all my intentions, and whispered, "Allah be praised," over and over, like a mindless person, or one so old his brain no longer functions, or a child, or a fool.

In truth, I remember little from all that transpired. Only this: that the wind blows a person back and forth across the rock at such speed the eye cannot focus on the surface, which is a gray blur; and that many times I struck the rock, jarring my bones, splitting my skin; and once I banged my head and saw brilliant white spots like stars before my eyes, and I thought I would be faint, but I was not. And in due time, which in truth seemed as the whole duration of my life, and more, I reached the bottom, and Buliwyf clapped me on the shoulder and said I had done well.

Now the sling was raised up; and the waves crashed over me and over Buliwyf at my side. Now I fought to hold my balance upon this slippery ledge, and this so occupied my attention I did not watch the others coming down the cliff. My only desire was this: to keep from being swept away into the sea. Verily I saw with my own eyes that the waves were taller than three men standing one atop another, and when each wave struck, I was for a moment senseless in a swirl of chilled water and spinning force. Many times was I knocked from my feet by these waves; I was drenched over my whole body, and shivering so badly that my teeth clattered like a galloping horse. I could not speak words for the clacking of my teeth.

Now all the warriors of Buliwyf made their descent; and all were safe, Ecthgow being the last to come down, by brute force of his arms, and when at last he stood, his legs quivered without control as a man shudders with a death throe; we waited some moments until he was himself again.

Then Buliwyf spoke: "We shall descend into the water and swim into the cave. I shall be first. Carry your dagger in your teeth, so your arms shall be free to battle the currents."

These words of new madness came upon me at a time when I could endure nothing further. To my eyes, the plan of Buliwyf was folly beyond folly. I saw the waves crash in, bursting upon the jagged rocks; I saw the waves pull away again with the tug of a giant's strength, only to recover their power and crash forward anew. Verily, I watched and I believed that no man could swim in that water, but rather he would be dashed to bony splinters in an instant.

But I made no protest, for I was past any comprehension. To my way of thinking, I was close enough to death that it did not matter if I came closer still. Thus I took my dagger, which I jammed into my belt, for my teeth rattled too severely to grip it in my mouth. Of the other Northmen, they gave no sign of coldness or fatigue, but rather greeted each wave as a fresh invigoration; also they smiled with the happy anticipation of the coming battle, and for this last I hated them.

Buliwyf watched the movement of the waves, choosing his time, and then he leapt into the surf. I hesitated, and some-one—I have always believed it to be Herger—pushed me. I fell deep in the swirling sea of numbing coldness; verily I was spun head over feet and sideward also; I could see no thing but green water. Then I perceived Buliwyf kicking down into the depths of the sea; and I followed after him, and he swam into a kind of passage in the rocks. In all things, I did as he did. This was the fashion:

Upon one moment, the surf would tug after him, trying to pluck him into the wide ocean, and me also. At these moments, Buliwyf gripped onto a rock with his hands to hold against the current; this also I did. Mightily I held to the rocks, with my lungs bursting. Then in an instant the surge ran opposite, and I was propelled with frightful speed forward, bouncing off rocks and obstructions. And then again, the surge changed, and tugged backward as it had done previously; and I was obliged to follow the example of Buliwyf and cling to rocks. Now it is true that my lungs burned as if afire, and I knew in my heart that I could not continue much longer in this icy sea. Then the surge ran forward, and I was flung headlong, knocked here and there, and then suddenly I was up and breathing air.

Verily this transpired with such swiftness that I was so surprised I did not think to feel relief, which was a proper feeling; nor did I think to praise Allah for my good fortune

in surviving. I gasped air, and all about me the warriors of
Buliwyf set their heads above the surface and gasped likewise.

Now, here is what I saw: we were in a kind of pond or
lake, inside a cave with a smooth rocky dome and a seaward
entrance through which we had just traversed. Directly
ahead was a flat rocky space. I saw three or four dark shapes
squatted about a fire; these creatures chanted in high voices.
Now also I understood why this was called the cave of
thunder, for with each crash of the surf the sound in the
cave reverberated with such power that the ears ached and
the very air seemed to shake and press.

In this place, this cave, Buliwyf and his warriors made
their attack, and I joined in with them, and with our short
daggers we killed the four demons in the cave. I saw them
clearly for the first time, in the flickering light of the fire,
whose flames leapt madly with each pounding of the thun-
dering surf. The aspect of these demons was thus: they
appeared to be manlike in every respect, but not as any man
upon the face of the earth. They were short creatures, and
broad and squat, and hairy on all parts of their bodies save
their palms, the soles of their feet, and their faces. Their
faces were very large, with mouth and jaws large and prominent, and of an ugly aspect; also their heads were larger
than the heads of normal men. Their eyes were sunk deep in
their heads; the brows were large, and not by virtue of hairy
brows, but of bone; also their teeth were large and sharp,
although it is true the teeth of many were ground down
and flattened.

In other respects of their bodily features and as to the

organs of sex and the several orifices, they were also as men.*
One of the creatures was slow to die, and with its tongue
formed some sounds, which had to my ear a quality of
speech; but I cannot know if this was so, and I tell it again
with no conviction of the matter.

Now Buliwyf surveyed these four dead creatures, with
their thick matted fur; then we heard a ghostly, echoing
chant, a sound rising and falling in time to the thunder
pounding of the surf, and this sound came from the recesses
of the cave. Buliwyf led us into the depths.

There we came upon three of the creatures, prostrate upon
the ground, faces pressed to the earth and their hands raised
in supplication to an old creature lurking in the shadows.
These suppliants were chanting, and did not perceive our
arrival. But the creature saw us, and screamed hideously at
our approach. This creature I took to be the mother of the
wendol, but if she was female, I saw no sign, for she was
old to the point of being sexless.

Buliwyf alone fell upon the suppliants and killed them
all, while the mother-creature moved back into the shadows
and screamed horribly. I could not see her well, but this
much is true: that she was surrounded by serpents, which
coiled at her feet, and upon her hands, and around her neck.
These serpents hissed and flicked their tongues; and as they
were all about her, upon her body and also on the ground,
none of the warriors of Buliwyf dared make an approach.

Then Buliwyf attacked her, and she gave a fearful scream
as he plunged his dagger deep into her breast, for he was

* This description of the physical features of the wendol has sparked
a predictable debate. See Appendix.

heedless of the snakes. Many times he struck the mother of the wendol with his dagger. Never did this woman collapse, but always did she stand, though the blood poured from her as if from a fountain, and from the several wounds Buliwyf inflicted upon her. And all the time she screamed a most frightful sound.

Then at the last she toppled, and lay dead, and Buliwyf turned to face his warriors. Now we saw that this woman, the mother of the eaters of the dead, had wounded him. A silver pin, such as a pin for hair, was buried in his stomach; this same pin trembled with each heartbeat. Buliwyf plucked it forth, and there was a gush of blood. Yet he did not sink to his knees mortally wounded, but rather he stood and gave the order to leave the cave.

This we did, by the second and landward entrance; this entrance had been guarded, but all the wendol guards had fled before the screams of their dying mother. We departed without harassment. Buliwyf led us from the caves, and back to our horses, and then did he collapse upon the ground.

Ecthgow, with a face of sadness most uncommon among the Northmen, directed the fashioning of a stretcher* and with this we carried Buliwyf back across the fields to the kingdom of Rothgar. And all the while Buliwyf was of good cheer, and merry; many of the things he spoke I did not comprehend, but one time I heard him say: "Rothgar will not be happy to see us, for he must set out yet another banquet, and by now he is a most depleted host." The warriors laughed at this and other words of Buliwyf. I saw their laughter was honest.

* *Lectulus.*

Now we came to the kingdom of Rothgar, where we were greeted with cheers and happiness, and no sadness, although Buliwyf was direly injured, and his flesh turned gray, and his body shook, and his eyes were lit by the gleam of a sick and fevered soul. These signs did I know full well, and so, too, did the North people.

A bowl of onion broth was brought for him, and he refused it, saying, "I have the soup illness; do not trouble yourselves on my account." Then he called for a celebration, and insisted that he preside over it, sitting propped up on a stone couch at the side of King Rothgar, and he drank mead and he was merry. I was near to him when he said to King Rothgar, in the midst of the festivities, "I have no slaves."

"All of my slaves are your slaves," Rothgar said.

Then Buliwyf said, "I have no horses."

"All of my horses are yours," Rothgar answered. "Think no more on these matters."

And Buliwyf, his wounds bound, was happy, and he smiled, and the color returned to his cheeks that evening, and indeed he seemed to grow stronger with each passing minute of the night. And although I would not have thought it possible, he ravished a slave girl, and afterward he said to me, as a joke, "A dead man is no use to anyone."

And then Buliwyf fell into a sleep, and his color became more pale and his breathing more shallow; I feared he should never awake from this sleep. He may also have thought this, for as he slept he held his sword gripped tight in his hand.

The death throes
of the wendol

So also I fell into a sleep. Herger awakened me
with these words: "You are to come quickly." Now I heard
the sound of distant thunder. I looked to the bladder
window* and it was not yet dawn, but I grabbed up my
sword; in truth I had fallen asleep in my armor, not caring
to remove it. Then I hastened outside. It was the hour before the dawn, and the air was misty and thick, and filled
with the thunder of distant hoofbeats.

Herger said to me, "The wendol come. They know of the
mortal wounds of Buliwyf, and they seek a final revenge for
the killing of their mother."

Each of the warriors of Buliwyf, myself among them,
took a place at the perimeter of the fortifications that we
had drawn up against the wendol. These defenses were
poor, yet we had none else. We peered into the mists to
glimpse the horsemen galloping down upon us. I expected
great fear, but I did not feel this, for I had seen the aspect of

---

* *Fenestra porcus:* literally, "pig window." The Norsemen used
stretched membranes instead of glass to cover narrow windows; these
membranes were translucent. One could not see much through them,
but light would be admitted into houses.

the wendol and knew them to be creatures, if not men, then like enough to men as monkeys are also like men; but I knew them to be mortal, and they could die.

Thus I had no fear, save the expectation of this final battle. In this manner was I alone, for I saw that the warriors of Buliwyf displayed much fear; and this despite their pains to conceal it. Verily, as we had killed the mother of the wendol, who was their leader, so also had we lost Buliwyf, who was our own leader, and there was no cheerfulness while we waited and heard the thunder approach.

And then I heard a commotion behind me, and upon my turning, I saw this: Buliwyf, pale as the mist itself, garbed in white and bound in his wounds, stood erect upon the land of the kingdom of Rothgar. And on his shoulders sat two black ravens, one to each side; and at this sight the North-men screamed of his coming, and they raised their weapons into the air and howled for the battle.*

* This section of the manuscript is pieced together from the manu-script of Razi, whose chief interest was military techniques. Whether or not Ibn Fadlan knew, or recorded, the significance of Buliwyf's reappearance is unknown. Certainly Razi did not include it, al-though the significance is obvious enough. In Norse mythology, Odin is popularly represented as bearing a raven on each shoulder. These birds bring him all the news of the world. Odin was the principal deity of the Norse pantheon and was considered the Universal Father. He ruled especially in matters of warfare; it was believed that from time to time he would appear among men, although rarely in his godlike form, preferring to assume the appearance of a simple traveler. It was said that an enemy would be scared away simply by his presence.

Interestingly, there is a story about Odin in which he is killed and resurrected after nine days; most authorities believe this idea ante-dates any Christian influence. In any case, the resurrected Odin was still mortal, and it was believed that he would someday finally die.

Now Buliwyf never spoke, nor did he look to one side or another; nor did he give sign of recognition to any man; but he walked with measured pace forward, beyond the line of the fortifications, and there he awaited the onslaught of the wendol. The ravens flew off, and he gripped his sword Runding and met the attack.

No words can describe the final attack of the wendol in the dawn of the mist. No words will say what blood was spilled, what screams filled the thick air, what horses and horsemen died in hideous agony. With my own eyes I saw Ecthgow, with his arms of steel: verily his head was lopped off by a wendol sword and the head bounced upon the ground as a bauble, the tongue still flicking in the mouth. Also I saw Weath take a spear through his chest; in this way was he pinned to the ground, and there writhed like a fish taken from the sea. I saw a girl child trampled by the hooves of a horse and her body crushed flat and blood pouring from her ear. Also I saw a woman, a slave of King Rothgar: her boy was cut in twain cleanly while she ran from a pursuing horseman. I saw many children likewise killed. I saw horses rear and plunge, their riders dismounted, to be fallen upon by old men and women, who slew the creatures as they lay stunned on their backs. Also I saw Wiglif, the son of Rothgar, run from the fray and conceal himself in cowardly safety. The herald I did not see that day.

I myself killed three of the wendol, and suffered a spear in the shoulder, which pain was like a plunge into fire; my blood boiled the length of my arm and also inside my chest; I thought I should collapse, and yet I fought on.

Now the sun burst through the mist, and the dawn was full upon us, and the mist slipped away, and the horsemen disappeared. In the broad light of day, I saw bodies everywhere, including many bodies of the wendol, for they had not collected their dead. This truly was the sign of their end, for they were in disarray and could not again attack Rothgar, and all the people of the kingdom of Rothgar knew this meaning and rejoiced.

Herger bathed my wound, and was elated, until they carried the body of Buliwyf into the great hall of Rothgar. Buliwyf was dead a score over: his body was hacked by the blades of a dozen adversaries; his visage and form was soaked in his own still-warm blood. Herger saw this sight and burst into tears, and hid his face from me, but there was no need, for I myself felt tears that misted my sight.

Buliwyf was laid before King Rothgar, whose duty it was to make a speech. But the old man was not able to do such a thing. He said only this: "Here is a warrior and a hero fit for the gods. Bury him as a great king," and then he left the hall. I believe he was ashamed, for he himself had not joined in the battle. Also his son Wiglif had run like a coward, and many had seen this, and called it a womanly act; this also may have abashed the father. Or there may be some reason which I do not know. In truth, he was a very old man.

Now it happened that in a low voice Wiglif spoke to the herald: "This Buliwyf has done us much service, all the greater for his death at the concluding of it." Thus he spoke when his father the King had departed the hall.

Herger heard these words, and I also did, and I was the

first to draw my sword. Herger said to me, "Do not battle this man, for he is a fox, and you have wounds."

I said to him, "Who cares for that?" and I challenged the son Wiglif, and upon the spot. Wiglif drew his sword. Now Herger delivered me a mighty kick or manner of blow from behind, and as I was unprepared for this I fell sprawling; then Herger joined battle with the son Wiglif. Also the herald took up arms, and moved slyly, in the desire to stand behind Herger and slay him at the back. This herald I myself killed by plunging my sword deep into his belly, and the herald screamed at the instant of his impalement. The son Wiglif heard this, and although he had battled fearlessly before, now he showed much fear in his contest with Herger.

Then it happened that King Rothgar heard of the clashing; he came once more to the great hall and begged for a ceasing of the matter. In this, his efforts were to no avail. Herger was firm in his purpose. Verily I saw him stand astride the body of Buliwyf and swing his sword at Wiglif, and Herger slew Wiglif, who fell down upon the table of Rothgar, and gripped the cup of the King, and drew it toward his lips. But it is true that he died without drinking, and so the matter was finished.

Now of the party of Buliwyf, once of the number thirteen, only four remained. I among them, we set out Buliwyf beneath a wooden roof, and left his body with a cup of mead in his hands. Then Herger said to the assembled people, "Who shall die with this noble man?" and a woman, a slave of King Rothgar, said that she would die with Buliwyf. The usual preparations of the Northmen were then made.

[Although Ibn Fadlan does not specify any passage of time,
several days probably elapsed before the funeral ceremony.]

Now a ship was fitted out upon the shore below the hall
of Rothgar, and treasures of gold and silver were laid upon
it, and the carcasses of two horses also. And a tent was
erected, and Buliwyf, now stiff in death, placed inside. His
body was the black color of death in this cold climate. Then
the slave girl was taken to each of the warriors of Buliwyf,
and to me also, and I had carnal knowledge of her, and she
said to me, "My master thanks you." Her countenance and
manner was most joyful, of a variety in excess of the general
good cheer these people show. Whilst she dressed again in
her garments, these garments including many splendid ornaments of gold and silver, I said to her that she was joyful.

I had in my mind that she was a fair maiden, and youth-
ful, and yet soon to die, which she knew, as did I. She said to
me, "I am joyful because I shall soon see my master." As yet
she had drunk no mead, and she spoke the truth of her heart.
Her countenance shone as does a happy child, or certain
women when they are with child; this was the nature of
the thing.

So, then, I said this: "Tell your master when you see him
that I have lived to write." These words I do not know if she
comprehended. I said to her, "It was the wish of your
master."

"Then I will tell him," she said, and most cheerfully
proceeded to the next warrior of Buliwyf. I do not know if
she understood my meaning, for the only sense of writing
these North people know is the carving of wood or stone,

which they do but seldom. Also, my speech in the North tongue was not clear. Yet she was cheerful and went on.

Now in the evening, as the sun was making its descent into the sea, the ship of Buliwyf was prepared upon the beach, and the maiden was taken into the tent of the ship, and the old crone who is called the angel of death placed the dagger between her ribs, and I and Herger held the cord that strangled her, and we seated her alongside Buliwyf, and then we departed.

All of this day I had taken no food or drink, for I knew I must participate in these affairs, and I had no wish to suffer the embarrassment of purging myself. But I felt no revulsion at any of the deeds of that day, nor was I faint, or light of head. For this I was proud in secret. Also it is true that at the moment of her death the maiden smiled, and this expression afterward remained, so that she sat next to her master with this same smile upon her pale face. The face of Buliwyf was black and his eyes were closed, but his expression was calm. Thus did I last view these two North people.

Now the ship of Buliwyf was set aflame, and pushed out into the sea, and the Northmen stood upon the rocky shore and made many invocations to their gods. With my own eyes, I saw the ship carried by the currents as a burning pyre, and then it was lost to vision, and the darkness of night descended upon the Northlands.

The return from
the North country

Now I passed some further weeks in the company
of the warriors and nobles of the kingdom of Rothgar. This
was a pleasant time, for the people were gracious and
hospitable, and most attentive to my wounds, which healed
well, praise Allah. But it happened soon enough that I desired to return to my own land. To King Rothgar I made
known that I was the emissary of the Caliph of Bagdad,
and that I must complete the business he had sent me upon,
or incur his wrath.

None of this mattered to Rothgar, who said I was a noble
warrior, that he desired I should remain in his lands, to live
the life of such an honored warrior. He said I was his friend
forevermore, and that I should have whatever I desired
within his means to give me. Yet he was reluctant to let me
depart, and contrived all manner of excuses and delays.
Rothgar said I must look to my wounds, although these injuries were plainly healed; also he said I must recover my
strength, although my strength was evidently restored. Finally he said I must await the outfitting of a ship, which
was no mean undertaking; and when I inquired after the
time such a ship might be outfitted, the King made a vague
reply, as if this did not matter to him overmuch. And upon

those times when I pressed him to depart, he turned cross and asked if I was dissatisfied with his hospitality; to this I was obliged to respond with praise for his graciousness and all variety of expressions of contentment. Soon enough I thought the old King less a fool than I had previously.

Now I went to Herger, speaking of my plight and I said to him: "This King is not such a fool as I have taken him to be."

In reply, Herger said: "You are wrong, for he is a fool, and does not act with sense." And Herger said he would arrange for my departure with the King.

Here was the manner of it. Herger sought the audience of King Rothgar in private, and said to the King that he was a great and wise ruler whose people loved and respected him, by virtue of the way that he looked after the affairs of the kingdom and the welfare of his people. This flattery softened the old man. Now Herger said to him that of the five sons of the King, only one survived, and he was Wulfgar, who had gone to Buliwyf as messenger, and now remained far off. Herger said that Wulfgar should be summoned home, and that a party for this purpose be arranged, for there was no other heir save Wulfgar.

These things he told the King. Also, I believe he spoke some words in private to the Queen Weilew, who had much influence over her husband.

Then it happened at an evening banquet that Rothgar called for the fitting out of a ship and a crew, for a voyage to return Wulfgar to his kingdom. I requested to join the crew, and this the old King could not deny me. The preparation of the ship took the space of several days. I spent much time with Herger in this interval. Herger had chosen to remain behind.

One day we stood upon the cliffs, overlooking the ship on the beach, as it was prepared for the voyage and fitted with provisions. Herger said to me: "You are starting upon a long journey. We shall make prayers for your safe-keeping."

I inquired whom he would pray to, and he responded, "To Odin, and Frey, and Thor, and Wyrd, and to the several other gods who may influence your safe journey." These are the names of the Northmen gods.

I replied, "I believe in one God, who is Allah, the All-Merciful and Compassionate."

"I know this," Herger said. "Perhaps in your lands, one god is enough, but not here; here there are many gods and each has his importance, so we shall pray to all of them on your behalf." I thanked him then, for the prayers of a non-believer are as good as they are sincere, and I did not doubt the sincerity of Herger.

Now, Herger had long known that I believed differently from him, but as the time of my departure drew close, he inquired many times again of my beliefs, and at unusual moments, thinking to catch me off my guard and learn the truth. I took his many questions as a form of test, as Buliwyf once tested my knowledge of writing. Always I answered him in the same way, thus increasing his perplexity.

One day he said to me, with no show that he had ever inquired previously: "What is the nature of your god Allah?"

I said to him, "Allah is the one God, who rules all things, sees all things, knows all things, and disposes all things." These words I had spoken before.

After a time, Herger said to me, "Do you never anger this Allah?"

I said: "I do, but He is all-forgiving and merciful."

Herger said: "When it suits his purposes?"

I said that this was so, and Herger considered my answer. Finally he said this, with a shaking head: "The risk is too great. A man cannot place too much faith in any one thing, neither a woman, nor a horse, nor a weapon, nor any single thing."

"Yet I do," I said.

"As you see best," Herger replied, "but there is too much that man does not know. And what man does not know, that is the province of the gods."

In this way I saw that he would never be persuaded to my beliefs, nor I to his, and so we parted. In truth, it was a sad leave-taking, and I was heavy-hearted to depart from Herger and the remainder of the warriors. Herger felt this also. I gripped his shoulder, and he mine, and then I set out upon the black ship, which carried me to the land of the Dans. As this ship with her stout crew slipped away from the shores of Venden, I had view of the gleaming rooftops of the great hall of Hurot, and, turning away, of the gray and vast ocean before us. Now it happened

[The manuscript ends abruptly at this point, the end of a transcribed page, with the final terse words "*nunc fit,*" and although there is clearly more to the manuscript, further pas-]

sages have not been discovered. This is, of course, the purest historical accident, but every translator has commented upon the odd appropriateness of this abrupt ending, which suggests the start of some new adventure, some new strange sight, that for the most arbitrary reasons of the past thousand years will be denied us.

APPENDIX

The Mist Monsters

As William Howells has emphasized, it is a rather rare event that causes any living animal to die in such a way that he will be preserved as a fossil for centuries to come. This is especially true of a small, fragile, ground-living animal such as man, and the fossil record of early men is remarkably scanty.

Textbook diagrams of "the tree of man" imply a certainty of knowledge that is misleading; the tree is pruned and revised every few years. One of the most controversial and troublesome branches of that tree is the one usually labeled "Neanderthal Man."

He takes his name from the valley in Germany where the first remains of his type were discovered in 1856, three years before the publication of Darwin's *Origin of Species*. The Victorian world was displeased with the skeletal remains, and emphasized the crude and brutish aspects of Neanderthal man, until now the very word is, in the popular imagination, synonymous with all that is dumb and bestial in human nature.

It was with a kind of relief that early scholars decided that Neanderthal man had "disappeared" about 35,000 years ago, to be replaced by Cro-Magnon man, whose skeletal remains were presumed to show as much delicacy, sensitivity, and intelligence as the Neanderthal skull showed monstrous brutishness. The general presumption was that the superior, modern Cro-Magnon man killed off the Neanderthals.

Now the truth of the matter is that we have very few good examples of Neanderthal man in our skeletal material—of more than eighty known fragments, only about a dozen are complete enough, or dated carefully enough, to warrant serious study. We cannot really say with any certainty how widespread a form he was, or what happened to him. And recent reexamination of the skeletal evidence has disputed the Victorian belief in his monstrous, semihuman appearance.

In their 1957 review, Straus and Cave wrote: "If he could be reincarnated and placed in a New York subway—provided he were bathed, shaved, and dressed in modern clothing—it is doubtful whether he would attract any more attention than some of its other denizens."

Another anthropologist has put it more plainly: "You might think he was tough-looking, but you wouldn't object to your sister marrying him."

From here, it is only a short step to what some anthropologists already believe: that Neanderthal man, as an anatomical variant of modern man, has never disappeared at all, but is still with us.

A reinterpretation of the cultural remains associated with Neanderthal man also supports a benign view of the fellow. Past anthropologists were highly impressed with the beauty and profusion of the cave drawings that first appear with the arrival of Cro-Magnon man; as much as any skeletal evidence, these drawings tended to reinforce the notion of a wonderful new sensibility replacing the quintessence of "brute benightedness."

But Neanderthal man was remarkable in his own right. His culture, called Mousterian—again, after a site, Le Moustier in France—is characterized by stoneworking of quite a high order, much superior to any earlier cultural level. And it is now recognized that Neanderthal man had bone tools as well.

Most impressive of all, Neanderthal man was the first of our ancestors to bury his dead ritually. At Le Moustier, a teenage boy was placed in a trench, in a sleeping position; he was provided with a supply of flint tools, a stone axe, and roasted meat. That these materials were for the use of the deceased in some afterlife is undisputed by most anthropologists.

There is other evidence of religious feeling: in Switzerland there is a shrine to the cave bear, a creature worshiped, respected, and also eaten. And at Shanidar Cave in Iraq, a Neanderthal was buried with flowers in the grave.

All this points to an attitude toward life and death, a self-conscious view of the world, which lies at the core of what we believe distinguishes thinking man from the rest of the animal world. On existing evidence, we must conclude this attitude was first displayed by Neanderthal man.

The general reassessment of Neanderthal man coincides with the rediscovery of Ibn Fadlan's contact with the "mist monsters"; his description of these creatures is suggestive of Neanderthal anatomy, and raises the question of whether the Neanderthal form did, in fact, disappear from the earth thousands of years ago, or whether these early men persisted into historic times.

Arguments based on analogies cut both ways. There are historical examples of a handful of people with technologically superior culture wiping out a more primitive society in a matter of years; that is largely the story of the European contact with the New World. But there are also examples of primitive societies existing in isolated areas, unknown to more advanced, civilized peoples nearby. Such a tribe was recently discovered in the Philippines.

Appendix

The academic debate on Ibn Fadlan's creatures can be neatly summarized by the viewpoints of Geoffrey Wrightwood, of Oxford University, and E. D. Goodrich, of the University of Philadelphia. Wrightwood says (1971): "The account of Ibn Fadlan provides us with a perfectly serviceable description of Neanderthal men, coinciding with the fossil record and our suppositions about the cultural level of these early men. We should accept it immediately, had we not already decided these men vanished without a trace some 30–40,000 years previously. We should remember that we only believe this disappearance because we have found no fossils of a later date, and the absence of such fossils does not mean that they do not, in fact, exist.

"Objectively, there is no *a priori* reason to deny that a group of Neanderthals might have survived very late in an isolated region of Scandinavia. In any case this assumption best fits the description of the Arabic text."

Goodrich, a paleontologist well known for his skepticism, takes the contrasting view (1972): "The general accuracy of Ibn Fadlan's reporting may tempt us to overlook certain excesses in his manuscript. These are several, and they arise either from cultural preconditioning, or from a storyteller's desire to impress. He calls the Vikings giants when they most certainly were not; he emphasizes the dirty, drunken aspects of his hosts, which less fastidious observers did not find striking. In his report of the so-called 'wendol,' he places great importance on their hairiness and brutish appearance when, in fact, they may not have been so hairy, or so brutish. They may simply have been a tribe of *Homo sapiens*, living in isolation and without the level of cultural attainment manifested by the Scandinavians.

"There is internal evidence, within the body of the Ibn Fadlan manuscript, to support the notion that the 'wendol' are actually *Homo sapiens*. The pregnant female figurines described by the Arab are highly suggestive of the prehistoric carvings and figurines to be found at the Aurignacian industry sites in France and of the Gravettian finds in Willendorf, Austria, Level 9. Both Aurignacian and Gravettian cultural levels are associated with essentially modern man, and not Neanderthal Man.

"We must never forget that to untrained observers, *cultural* differences are often interpreted as *physical* differences, and one need not be particularly naïve to make this mistake. Thus, as late as the 1880's it was possible for educated Europeans to wonder aloud whether Negroes in primitive African societies could be considered human beings at all, or whether they represented some bizarre mating of men and apes. Nor should we overlook the degree to which societies with vastly differing degrees of cultural attainment may exist side by side; such contrasts appear today, for example, in Australia, where the stone age and the jet age can be found in close proximity. Thus in interpreting the descriptions of Ibn Fadlan we need not postulate a Neanderthal remnant, unless we are fancifully inclined to do so."

In the end, the arguments stumble over a well-known limitation to the scientific method itself. The physicist Gerhard Robbins observes that "strictly speaking, no hypothesis or theory can ever be proven. It can only be disproven. When we say we believe a theory, what we really mean is that we are unable to show that the theory is wrong—not that we are able to show, beyond doubt, that the theory is right.

"A scientific theory may stand for years, even centuries, and it may accumulate hundreds of bits of corroborating evidence to support it. Yet a theory is always vulnerable, and a single conflicting finding is all that is required to throw the hypothesis into disarray, and call for a new theory. One can never know when such conflicting evidence will arise. Perhaps it will happen tomorrow, perhaps never. But the history of science is strewn with the ruins of mighty edifices toppled by an accident, or a triviality."

Appendix

This is what Geoffrey Wrightwood meant when he said at the Seventh International Symposium on Human Paleontology in Geneva in 1972: "All I need is one skull, or a fragment of a skull, or a bit of jaw. In fact, all I need is one good tooth, and the debate is concluded."

Until that skeletal evidence is found, speculation will continue, and one may adopt whatever stance satisfies an inner sense of the fitness of things.

SOURCES

I. Primary Sources

Yakut ibn-Abdallah MS, a geographical lexicon, ?A.D. 1400.
Nos. 1403A–1589A, Archives University Library, Oslo, Norway.
    Trans: Blake, Robert, and Frye, Richard; in *Byzantina—Meta-*
        byzantina: A Journal of Byzantine and Modern Greek
        Studies, New York, 1947.
        Cook, Albert S.; New York, 1947.
        Fraus-Dolus, Per; Oslo, 1959–1960.
        Jorgensen, Olaf; 1971, unpublished.
        Nasir, Seyed Hossein; 1971, unpublished.

St. Petersburg MS, a local history, published by the Academy
of St. Petersburg, 1823. Nos. 233M–278M, Archives University
Library, Oslo, Norway.
    Trans: Fraus-Dolus, Per; Oslo, 1959–1960.
        Stenuit, Roger; 1971, unpublished.
        Soletsky, V. K.; 1971, unpublished.

Ahmad Tusi MS, a geography, A.D. 1047, papers of J. H. Emerson. Nos. LV 01–114, Archives University Library, Oslo, Norway.
    Trans: Fraus-Dolus, Per; Oslo, 1959–1960.
        Nasir, Seyed Hossein; 1971, unpublished.
        Hitti, A. M.; 1971, unpublished.

Sources

Amin Razi MS, a history of warfare, A.D. 1585–1595, papers of J. H. Emerson. Nos. LV 207–244, Archives University Library, Oslo, Norway.

Trans: Fraus-Dolus, Per; Oslo, 1959–1960.

Bendixon, Robert; 1971, unpublished.

Porteus, Eleanor; 1971, unpublished.

Xymos MS, a fragmentary geography, ? date, bequest estate A. G. Gavras. Nos. 2308T–2348T, Archives University Library, Oslo, Norway.

Trans: Fraus-Dolus, Per; Oslo, 1959–1960.

Bendixon, Robert; 1971, unpublished.

Porteus, Eleanor; 1971, unpublished.

II. Secondary Source

Berndt, E. and Berndt, R. H. "An Annotated Bibliography of References to the Manuscript of Ibn Fadlan from 1794 to 1970," *Acta Archaeologica,* VI: 334–389, 1971.

This remarkable compilation will refer the interested reader to all secondary sources concerning the manuscript, which have appeared in English, Norwegian, Swedish, Danish, Russian, French, Spanish, and Arabic for the dates cited. The total number of sources listed is 1,042.

III. General Reference Works

The following are suitable for the general reader with no particular archaeological or historical background. Only works in English are cited.

Wilson, D. M.   *The Vikings,* London, 1970.
Brondsted, J.   *The Vikings,* London, 1960, 1965.

Sources

Arbman, H. *The Vikings,* London, 1961.

Jones, G. *A History of the Vikings,* Oxford, 1968.

Sawyer, P. *The Age of the Vikings,* London, 1962.

Foote, P. G., and Wilson, D. M. *The Viking Achievement,* London, 1970.

Kendrick, T. D. *A History of the Vikings,* London, 1930.

Azhared, Abdul. *Necronomicon* (ed. H. P. Lovecraft), Providence, Rhode Island, 1934.

A FACTUAL NOTE ON
EATERS OF THE DEAD

Eaters of the Dead was conceived on a dare. In 1974, my friend Kurt Villadsen proposed to teach a college course he called "The Great Bores". The course would include all the texts that were supposed to be crucial to Western civilization but which were, in truth, no longer read willingly by anyone, because they were so tedious. Kurt said that the first of the great bores he would address was the epic poem *Beowulf*.

I disagreed. I argued that *Beowulf* was a dramatic, exciting story—and that I could prove it. I went home and immediately began making notes for this novel.

I started from the scholarly tradition that examined epic poetry and mythology as if it might have some underlying basis in fact. Heinrich Schliemann assumed the *Iliad* was true, and found what he claimed was Troy and Mycenae; Arthur Evans believed there was something to the myth of the Minotaur, and uncovered the Palace of Knossos on Crete;[1] M. I. Finley and others had traced the route of Ulysses in the *Odyssey*;[2] Lionel Casson had written about the real journeys that might underlie the myth of Jason and the Argonauts.[3] Thus it seemed reasonable, within this

---

[1] The classic popular account of Evans and Schliemann is C. W. Ceram (Kurt W. Merek), *Gods Graves and Scholars*, Alfred A. Knopf, New York, 1967.
[2] M. I. Finley, *The World of Odysseus*, Viking Press, New York, 1965.
[3] Lionel Casson, *The Ancient Mariners, Sea Farers and Sea Fighters of the Mediterranean in Ancient Times*, Macmillan, New York, 1959.

tradition, to imagine that *Beowulf*, too, had originally been based on an actual event.

That event had been embellished over centuries of oral retelling, producing the fantastic narrative we read today. But I thought it might be possible to reverse the process, peeling away the poetic invention, and returning to a kernel of genuine human experience—something that had actually happened.

This idea of uncovering the factual core of the narrative was appealing but impractical. Modern scholarship offered no objective procedure to separate poetic invention from underlying fact. Even to try would mean making innumerable subjective decisions, large and small, on every page—in the end, so many decisions that the results must inevitably be still another invention: a modern pseudo-historical fantasy about what the original events might have been.

The insoluble problem prevented me from proceeding. Of course, in writing a novel, I intended to create a fantasy of my own. But fantasies demand strict logic, and I was troubled by the logic behind what I wanted to write. Since a real scholar could not do what I intended to do, I found I could not pretend, in writing, that I had done so. This was not a failure of imagination or nerve. It was a purely practical problem. Like the scholar, I had no basis for deciding which elements of the *Beowulf* narrative to keep, and which to discard.

Although the idea of working backward seemed untenable, I remained intrigued. I asked a different question: suppose, for a moment, that the practical problems that troubled me did not exist, and the process could indeed be carried out. What would the resulting narrative look like? I imagined it would probably be a rather mundane recounting of some battles that occurred more than a thousand years ago. In fact, I suspected it would probably resemble most eyewitness accounts of famous events, as written by people who are unaware of the significance of the events they are seeing.

This line of thinking eventually led to the solution to my

problem. Clearly, I wanted an eyewitness account. I could not extract it from the existing *Beowulf* narrative, and I did not want to invent it. That was my impasse. But at some point, I realized I did not have to invent it—I could *discover* it instead.

Suppose, I thought, a contemporary observer had been present at these battles, and had written an account of the events that were later transformed into a poem. Suppose, too, that this account *already existed*, but had never been recognized for what it was. If this were so, then no invention on my part would be necessary. I could merely reproduce the eyewitness narrative, and annotate it for the reader.

The concept of a preexisting manuscript bypassed the logical problems which had earlier impeded me, because a found manuscript would not be my creation—even though I would create it. Of course such thinking is absurd, but it happens all the time. Often actors cannot act without a prop, or a false moustache, or some other artifice to separate themselves from the character they are portraying. I was engaged in a similar process.

What sort of narrative would be most desirable? I concluded the most useful account would be written by an outsider— someone not part of the culture, who could report objectively on the events as they occurred. But who would this outside observer have been? Where would he have come from?

On reflection, I realized I already knew of such a person. In the tenth century, an Arab named Ibn Fadlan had travelled north from Baghdad into what is now Russia, where he came in contact with the Vikings. His manuscript, well-known to scholars, provides one of the earliest eyewitness accounts of Viking life and culture.[4] As a college undergraduate, I had read portions of the

---

[4]Among the many discussions of Viking society for the general reader, see: D. M. Wilson, *The Viking*, London, 1970; J. Brondsted, *The Vikings*, London, 1965; P. Sawyer, *The Age of the Vikings*, London, 1962; P. G. Foote and D. M. Wilson, *The Viking Achievement*, London, 1970. Some of these references quote passages from Ibn Fadlan's manuscript.

manuscript. Ibn Fadlan had a distinct voice and style. He was imitable. He was believable. He was unexpected. And after a thousand years, I felt that Ibn Fadlan would not mind being revived in a new role, as a witness to the events that led to the epic poem of *Beowulf.*

Although the full manuscript of Ibn Fadlan has been translated into Russian, German, French and many other languages, only portions had been translated into English. I obtained the existing manuscript fragments and combined them, with only slight modifications, into the first three chapters of *Eaters of the Dead.*[5] I then wrote the rest of the novel in the style of the manuscript to carry Ibn Fadlan on the rest of his now-fictional journey. I also added commentary and some extremely pedantic footnotes.

I was aware that Ibn Fadlan's actual journey in A.D. 921 had probably occurred too late in history to serve as the basis for *Beowulf,* which many authorities believe was composed a hundred and fifty years earlier. But the dating of the poem is uncertain, and at some point a novelist will insist on his right to take liberties with the facts. And *Eaters* contains many overt anachronisms, particularly when Ibn Fadlan meets up with a group of remnant Neanderthals. (One of the oddities of this book is that the intervening decades has seen a scholarly reevaluation of Neanderthal man; and the notion that there might have been a few still around a thousand years ago in remote location does not seem quite so preposterous now as it did then.)

[5]To my knowledge there are still only two principal sources in English. The first is the text fragments I read as an undergraduate: Robert Blake and Richard Frye, "The Vikings Abroad and at Home," in Carleton S. Coon, *A Reader in General Anthropology,* Henry Holt and Co. NY, 1952, pp. 410–416. The second source is Robert P. Blake and Richard N. Frye. "Notes on the Risala of Ibn-Fadlan," *Byzantina Metabyzantina,* 1949, v. 1 part 2, New York, pp. 7–37. I am grateful to Professor Frye for his assistance during the first publication of this book, and this recent revision.

A *Factual Note on* Eaters of the Dead

But certainly, the game that the book plays with its factual bases becomes increasingly complex as it goes along, until the text finally seems quite difficult to evaluate. I have a long-standing interest in verisimilitude, and in the cues which make us take something as real or understand it as fiction. But I finally concluded that in *Eaters of the Dead*, I had played the game too hard. While I was writing, I felt that I was drawing the line between fact and fiction clearly; for example, one cited translator, Per Fraus-Dolus, means in literal Latin "by trickery-deceit." But within a few years, I could no longer be certain which passages were real, and which were made up; at one point I found myself in a research library trying to locate certain references in my bibliography, and finally concluding, after hours of frustrating effort, that however convincing they appeared, they must be fictitious. I was furious to have wasted my time, but I had only myself to blame.

I mention this because the tendency to blur the boundaries of fact and fiction has become widespread in modern society. Fiction is now seamlessly inserted in everything from scholarly histories to television news. Of course, television is understood to be venal, its transgressions shrugged off by most of us. But the attitude of "post-modern" scholars represents a more fundamental challenge. Some in academic life now argue seriously there is no difference between fact and fiction, that all ways of reading text are arbitrary and personal, and that therefore pure invention is as valid as hard research. At best, this attitude evades traditional scholarly discipline; at worst, it is nasty and dangerous.[6] But such academic views were not prevalent twenty years ago, when I sat down to write this novel in the guise of a scholarly monograph, and academic fashions may change again—particularly if scholars find themselves chasing down imaginary footnotes, as I have done.

[6]For trends in post-modern academic thought, see for example Pauline Marie Rosenau, *Post-Modernism and the Social Sciences: Insights, Inroads, and Intrutions*, Princeton, New Jersey, 1992; and H. Aram Veser, ed., *The New Historicism*, Routledge, New York, 1989.

A *Factual Note on* Eaters of the Dead

Under the circumstances, I should perhaps say explicitly that the references in this afterword are genuine. The rest of the novel, including its introduction, text, footnotes, and bibliography, should properly be viewed as fiction.

When *Eaters of the Dead* was first published, this playful version of *Beowulf* received a rather irritable reception from reviewers, as if I had desecrated a monument. But *Beowulf* scholars all seem to enjoy it, and many have written to say so.

M.C.
DECEMBER, 1992